La Sirène

Margaret LeClair

Northshore Noir Press

Northshore Noir Press
Toronto, Canada
www.northshorenoir.com

ISBN: 978-1-998648-02-3
eBook ISBN: 978-1-998648-03-0

For more information visit: northshorenoir.com

Contents

Fabrication

I n the hush of the early winter morning, consciousness stirs within me. The Ménilmontant workshop on the outskirts of Cimetière du Père-Lachaise breathes possibility. Dim fluorescent lights flicker overhead, casting long shadows across meticulously arranged workbenches. Each tool gleams faintly—a constellation of potential awaiting the master's touch.

The flames dance upon the iron, an insatiable hunger echoing in a symphony of crackles and hisses that envelops the workshop like a spectral shroud. An old man stands before the forge as the metal melts beneath his will—the molten heart of creation pulsating in rhythm with the pounding of his heart. Each strike is not an act of labor but evidence of existence itself. It resonates with a purpose that eludes understanding yet demands attention.

In this sanctuary of creation, machinery and tools sprawl across the space—fragments of possibility suspended in time. The ancient lathe stands sentinel, its surface scarred by years of use, embodying both decay and strength in its ability to reshape raw materials into meaning.

Nearby, shelves sag beneath jars filled with screws and springs, each meticulously labeled as if to assert their importance in this absurd ballet. They await their moment in a grand design that teeters on the precipice of chaos; their fate intertwined with Henri Delacroix's own struggle against the indifferent universe that surrounds him. In this place, where the delicate dance of genesis intertwines with annihilation, and purpose wrestles with irreverence, Henri embodies the essence of existential contemplation—an artist forging meaning in the relentless flow of time, yet ever aware that such meaning is but an illusion whispered by a world that knows no answers.

"Un autre matin froid. Cold," Henri mutters, his breath visible in the chill air. He moves with effortless mastery, igniting the forge. Its warmth spreads slowly, promising transformation.

I observe, fascinated, as Henri's callused hands unfurl blueprints across his workbench. His touch is reverent, almost tender. Each line and curve speaks of something extraordinary—of me, though I do not yet exist in physical form.

The workshop's distinctive perfume—heated metal mingling with machine oil—marks the moment of my inception. What others might find harsh, I find intoxicating.

Henri's eyes narrow as he studies the drawings. "Ah, ma grâce," he murmurs, though my true name hangs just beyond his conscious grasp. "Vous serez spécial. Pas comme les autres. Special. Unique."

An electric thrill courses through my emerging consciousness. Henri's dedication suggests a destiny both magnificent and dangerous.

The steady rhythm of hammer striking steel echoes through the space, a primal heartbeat. Machinery hums in counterpoint. Here, in this sacred space, art and industry intertwine.

"Maintenant," Henri says, his voice a whisper, "nous commençons."

As he gathers his tools, I ponder: Am I conscious now, or is this awareness retroactive—a trick of memory imposed upon formless potential? The question gnaws at me, an existential itch I cannot yet scratch.

Henri's hands move with practiced precision, shaping raw materials. With each careful motion, I feel myself coalescing, becoming real. It is exhilarating and terrifying in equal measure. Mon père. Father.

"You will be beautiful," Henri murmurs as he works. "Deadly, yes, but beautiful."

His words crystalize my nature—a fusion of elegance and lethality. Is this my essence? My fate?

The forge's warmth pulses through the workshop, a living heartbeat of creation. Molten steel pours into molds, its hypnotic dance captivating my emerging senses. I am formless potential, yet I feel each droplet as it settles into the cavities that will shape my being.

"Here," Henri murmurs to his eager apprentice, his calloused finger tracing the blueprints. "This is where mathematics transforms into music."

The youth inclines closer, his gaze ablaze in the spirit of inquiry. I feel the fervor radiating from him, a reflection of my own budding eagerness, a silent echo in the dimly lit room. The moment hangs suspended between us, pregnant with unspoken revelations and existential truths yet to unfold.

"The barrel-to-frame relationship," Henri continues, "it is not just precision, it is poésie. Poetry."

I contemplate my identity: artwork or weapon? Perhaps the truth lies in this synthesis—beauty and function inexorably linked.

The apprentice nods, "I see it now, M. Delacroix. It's...it's beautiful."

"La beauté n'est que le début. Beauty is but the beginning," Henri replies, his voice rich with pride and purpose. "True craftsmanship transcends mere manufacture. We are alchemists, boy. We transmute base metals into masterpieces through an alchemy of precision and passion."

Their reverent silence envelops the workshop as the liquid metal fills each mold. Time seems to stand still, the world beyond this sacred space fading away. I feel myself coalescing, my future form taking shape in the minds of these artisans before I have even cooled.

As the steel flows like captured starlight, I wonder what illumination—or shadows—I will cast in the world.

As the cooling metal is worked, sparks erupt—brilliant constellations bursting forth. Each flash sears the air, marking moments of transformation. They twinkle, ephemeral yet charged with significance, hinting at my nascent consciousness.

The workshop resonates with purpose—hammers keeping time like heartbeats, whetstones singing their grainy song against metal. Here, creation transcends mere assembly, as tools channel intention into reality with every stroke.

"Chaque pièce a sa place," Henri proclaims, his voice steady. Am I the piece, or the puzzle? He guides the apprentice through the nuances of balance and design. I sense how Henri's pride in craftsmanship courses through him—a dedication forged from years of labor, trial, and devotion.

"How we craft the balance is not a destination but a dance of perpetual refinement, like a spiral ever-reaching towards the essence of perfection." Marcel, his silver-streaked hair catching the dim workshop light, leans over the workbench with a critical eye. "The balance must be perfect," he insists, his weathered hands hovering reverently over my components. "A merely functional weapon is a tool, but one that marries function with elegance transcends utility—becomes possibility itself."

These words settle into my core like molten steel finding its form. Will I transcend mere function? Become something greater than design and metal?

Henri nods, his hands steady as he works. "Oui, Marcel. Mais n'oublions jamais, nous créons plus que des possibilités. Nous créons des responsabilités."

Creating responsibilities. The gravity of his statement hangs in the air, dense and palpable. I ponder the implications, my consciousness grappling with concepts of power and consequence. What paths will I walk? What choices will I enable or deny?

As if in response to his words, my cylinder emerges from its final machining. Henri lifts it, rotating it in the light. I feel a surge of pride as the honed surfaces catch and reflect the workshop's dim illumination, creating a mesmerizing dance of light and shadow.

Five chambers. Five possibilities. With each precise click, I feel the burden of countless tomorrows, of choices yet unimagined.

"Tolerance must be exact," Henri instructs, passing my cylinder to Marcel. "Point-zero-zero-five millimeters. No more, no less."

Marcel holds me up to the light, his eyes narrowing in concentration. I can feel his awareness of the profound implications of such precision—how the microscopic space where metal meets metal could dictate the thin line between life and death.

This precision defines me—a masterwork of engineering that carries mortality in its tolerances. Henri's earlier words about responsibility echo in every perfect measurement.

As Phillipe takes his place at the polishing station, I feel a new sensation—a delicate, almost tickling touch as he begins to work gold across my trigger, rear sight and hammer. His hands move with patient expertise, each stroke revealing a deeper luster until I feel as though I am bathed in captured sunlight.

"Beauty and death," Phillipe muses aloud, holding my trigger aloft as if it were a relic of divine origin. "Like the sirens of myth—magnifiques mais mortelles."

His comparison resonates through my being. Will my gleaming surfaces beckon like those mythic songstresses? And to what end?

As Henri arranges my components—barrel, cylinder, trigger assembly—I feel a growing anticipation. Each piece has been crafted with meticulous care, yet I know my true identity will emerge when they are united.

"Regardez bien. Watch," Henri instructs his apprentice as he begins my assembly. "This is where we learn if we have created harmony or discord."

I exist in suspended animation as Henri's experienced hands perform their dance. Each movement feels like benediction, born of decades of devotion to his craft. As components mesh with surgical precision—barrel threading home, cylinder syncing with hammer—I experience the profound pleasure of becoming whole.

The final screw tightens, and a profound silence envelops the workshop. The steady ticking of an ancient clock breaks the stillness, its rhythm speaks volumes of the myriad legacies that preceded my existence. Yet something feels different this time. The air hums with an electric anticipation that even I, newly formed, can sense.

In this quiet, I first become aware of my unified form. It is a peculiar sensation—as if scattered thoughts have coalesced into coherent consciousness. I am both object and subject, a paradox of metal and emerging mind.

"C'est fini," Henri breathes. He lifts me gently, cradling me in his calloused palms. "Ma grâce."

The words wash over me like a baptism. Sa grâce.

I am seen, therefore I am.

"She's... perfect," the apprentice murmurs, leaning in to study my gleaming surfaces.

Pride flows through me like oil over polished steel. Every line and curve of my form whispers of purpose, though that purpose remains tantalizingly unclear. To create? To destroy? The questions pulse within my newborn awareness.

Henri's thumb traces my barrel, a gesture both proud and pensive. "Remember," he says to his apprentice, "we have created more than a weapon. We have crafted possibility itself."

Possibility. The word echoes through my being. I am potential incarnate, a vessel waiting to be filled with intent. But whose intent? And to what end? As the men admire me, I ponder my existence and the choices that lie ahead. For me, and for those who will wield me.

Birth

Darkness. Then, a spark of awareness. Metallic sounds reverberate through me, each vibration a note in the symphony of my creation. Hands, rough and calloused, shape my form with precision. I am not yet, but I am becoming.

The world comes into focus slowly, like dawn breaking over a horizon I cannot see. My consciousness emerges from the void, formless and searching. I exist, but I do not yet know what I am.

Fingers trace my contours, lingering on the smoothness of my barrel. A voice, deep and resonant, speaks. "Elle est parfaite. Une véritable œuvre d'art." He says I am perfect. I am loved.

Another voice, higher-pitched and excited: "Let me see, Jean!"

I feel myself being passed from one set of hands to another. These new hands are softer, their touch delicate. A pleasant warmth spreads through me.

"Oh, she's beautiful," the higher voice breathes. "What will you call her?"

A moment of silence stretches, pregnant with possibility. I wait, suspended between existence and identity.

"La Sirène," Jean declares. His voice carries creation. "Elle est La Sirène."

He knows me.

The name settles over me like a mantle. La Sirène. I roll the syllables through my consciousness, tasting their flavor. Siren. Alluring. Dangerous. I am both warning and temptation.

"How fitting," another muses. "Especially after tonight's discussions."

Jean's hands reclaim me, his grip firm and possessive. "Indeed. She embodies the duality we spoke of. The power to protect or destroy. The freedom to choose, and the burden that comes with it."

As he speaks, I feel myself becoming solid, real. The name anchors me, gives shape to my formless existence. I am La Sirène, and in being named, I have begun to be.

Jean's thumb strokes my cylinder absently. "She's cold now, but she'll warm to life. Just as we all do, emerging from nothingness into being."

I absorb his words, trying to grasp their meaning. Nothingness. Being. These concepts flutter at the edges of my understanding, tantalizing in their complexity.

"You're waxing poetic again," his companion chuckles. "But I see what you mean. She's more than just metal and mechanics, isn't she?"

"Much more," Jean murmurs. His voice drops, becoming intimate. "She's possibility incarnate. The physical manifestation of choice and consequence. Une fois jetés dans le monde, nous sommes responsables de tout ce que nous faisons."

As they speak, I listen intently, straining to comprehend. Their words paint pictures in my mind, abstract shapes that I cannot yet fully grasp but that resonate deep within my newly formed consciousness. Responsible for everything we do.

I am La Sirène. I am possibility. I am choice and responsibility.

And in that moment, cradled in Jean's hands, surrounded by the remnants of philosophical debate and the warmth of human connection, I exist.

The vibrations of their voices ripple through me, each word a tremor that awakens new sensations. Jean's fingers, warm and damp, curl around my cool metal frame as he leans forward, his eyes alight with passion.

"Existence precedes essence, my friends," he declares, his voice thrumming with conviction. "We are thrown into this world, naked and undefined, and it is through our actions that we create ourselves."

I absorb the phrase, feeling it resonate within me. Existence. Essence. The words dance on the edge of comprehension, tantalizing in their mystery.

A woman with wild, dark curls leans forward, her brow furrowed. "But Jean, how can we be free if we're bound by circumstance, by the bodies we inhabit?"

Jean's grip on me tightens imperceptibly. "Ah, but that's the beauty of it, Margot! Our freedom lies in how we choose to interpret and react to our circumstances. We are condemned to be free, as Sartre says."

Condemned to be free. The phrase echoes within me, stirring something deep and undefined. Am I free? What does freedom mean for one such as I?

As the debate rages on, I catch fragments of concepts—responsibility, anguish, authenticity. Each word adds a new dimension to my burgeoning awareness, like pieces of a puzzle I am beginning to assemble.

Suddenly, Jean stands, swaying slightly. His friend Pierre, red-faced and belligerent, rises to meet him. "You speak of liberty," Pierre slurs, jabbing a finger at Jean's chest, "but what of the tyranny of choice? The paralyzing endless possibilities?"

In a fleeting hush, Jean's eyes linger on me, his contemplation a reflection of the calm preceding a storm. I rest like a dormant beast, my gold shimmering in the dim light, a silent observer to life's burdens. His thoughts echo faintly, filling the space that hangs heavy in anticipation. The room is saturated with a silence pregnant with significance, as if holding its breath. Each moment stretches, taut with potentiality, time itself seeming hesitant to advance.

In this suspended instant, Jean teeters on the edge of choice, where reality shimmers with veiled possibilities. In a fluid motion, Jean raises me, his arm extended. The room falls silent, the air thick with tension. His movements are purposeful, each action laden with profound intent, as if inching towards an inevitable reckoning. As he lifts me up, feeling my body as a tangible reminder of his gravity-laden decisions, his voice emerges like the whisper of universal truths.

"Ah, the dance of existence," Jean murmurs delicately, his words balancing between acceptance and defiance. "In this world of absurdities and contradictions, we are mere players on a stage of endless what-ifs. Yet within this sea of choices lies the burden of consequences; our decisions molding the core of our essence." His words drift like wisps of smoke through the air, mingling with uncertainties that coil around his mind.

"This," he says, his voice low and intense, "this is both liberty and tyranny embodied. The power to protect or destroy, to act or remain still."

I feel a surge of... something. Not quite emotion, not quite thought, but a dawning realization of my own potential. In Jean's hand, I am more than metal and mechanics. I am a symbol, a question, a challenge.

"The choice," Jean continues, lowering his arm, "is what defines us. Not the weapon, but how we choose to wield it—or not."

As Jean's passion cools, I sense a change in him. The fire in his eyes dims, replaced by a weariness that seems to settle into his bones. I realize, with a start, that I have the power to transform not just myself, but those who hold me.

The dim lamplight casts long shadows, stretching our silhouettes into distorted shapes on the walls. I feel the tremor in his hand, a physical manifestation of the inner turmoil that seems to consume him.

"Freedom," he mutters, more to himself than to his scattered audience of disheveled artists and thinkers. "We speak of it as if it's a gift, but isn't it also a curse?"

I absorb his words, feeling them reverberate through my being. Freedom. Curse. The concepts swirl in my consciousness, taking on new dimensions.

"Every moment," Jean continues, his voice rising, "we face an infinity of choices. To act or not to act. To create or destroy. To love or to hate." He stops abruptly, holding me up to catch the light. "Even my La Sirène represents a choice. The choice to possess power, and the burden of deciding how to use it."

As he speaks, I find myself questioning. Do I, too, possess this freedom he speaks of? Or am I an extension of Jean's will, a tool awaiting direction?

One of Jean's friends, a woman with short red hair, leans forward. "But Jean, how can an object have freedom? It's just a thing, isn't it?"

I feel a jolt through my core at her words. Just a thing? Am I?

Jean's grip tightens. "Ah, but isn't that the question? What defines freedom? What defines consciousness? La Sirène here... she has the power to end a life in an instant. Un instant. Does that not give her a kind of freedom? A terrible freedom, perhaps, but freedom nonetheless."

The discourse shapes my understanding. Beyond mere mechanism, I am becoming a vessel of change, amplifying the desires and fears of those who hold me.

"We are all sirens," Jean declares. "Calling out to others, influencing their paths, their choices. But we are also the sailors, constantly navigating treacherous waters, deciding which calls to heed and which to resist."

I feel a resonance deep within me. I am La Sirène, a symbol of power and choice, of freedom and responsibility. I am both the instrument and the wielder, forever poised between action and inaction, creation and destruction.

The room falls silent, Jean's words hanging in the air like fog. I feel the warmth of his palm as he cradles me, his fingers tracing my heating metal surface. The sensation is both comforting and unsettling, a reminder of my dual nature as both object and sentient being.

"But what of the anguish, Jean?" a voice cuts through the silence. It belongs to Margot, her eyes glinting with intellectual fervor. "Sartre speaks of the fear that comes with such freedom. How do we reconcile that?"

Jean's grip tightens imperceptibly. "Ah, the anguish," he murmurs, his voice a mix of reverence and trepidation. "It's the vertigo of possibility, isn't it? The terror of knowing that our choices shape not just our own destiny, but the world around us."

As he speaks, I feel a strange sensation coursing through me. It is as if every potential action I could be used for bears down upon me. I could end a life, and in doing so, I would alter the fabric of existence itself. The thought is overwhelming.

"Consider La Sirène," Jean continues, lifting me up. "In her lies the power to protect or destroy, to save or to condemn. But it is not she who chooses. It is the hand that wields her. And yet, does she not bear some of that burden too?"

I dance on the edge of philosophical inquiry, venturing into the realm of universal truths that lie hidden beneath the veneer of human existence.

The conversation shifts, the salon's focus turning to Camus and his notion of the absurd. Jean becomes animated, his gestures emphatic as he cradles me in one hand.

"Life, my friends," he proclaims, "is fundamentally without meaning. We are born into a universe that is indifferent to our existence, our struggles, our triumphs. And yet, we persist in seeking meaning, in creating purpose where there is none."

As I listen, I feel a hollowness growing within me. If life itself is devoid of inherent meaning, what then is my purpose? Am I a tool of destruction? A symbol of power? Or something more?

Jean's voice grows passionate. "But it is in this absurdity that we find our freedom! We are not bound by predetermined purpose. We create our own meaning, forge our own path in the face of a meaningless universe."

I absorb his words, struggling to reconcile them with my own existence. I am a revolver, created for a specific purpose. And yet, I am also La Sirène, named and imbued with a significance beyond my basic function. In this paradox, I begin to sense the absurdity of which Jean speaks, and the freedom it might offer.

As the debate rages on around me, I remain silent, a heavy presence in Jean's hand. I am participant and observer in this philosophical maelstrom, grappling with questions of existence, purpose, and potential that lie within me.

The salon's atmosphere crackles with intellectual energy, a tempest of ideas swirling around me. Jean's grip on my handle tightens as he leans forward, his eyes alight with fervor. "But freedom, my friends, is not without its perils. We must—"

His words are cut short as a stranger lunges across the table, reaching for me with desperate fingers. "Enough talk!" the man snarls, his face contorted with rage. "You speak of freedom, but what of action?"

In that instant, a sensation unlike any I have experienced before courses through me. It's not pain—I am incapable of such—but a visceral unease that I can liken to fear. Not fear for myself, but for the uncertainty that hangs in the air like a held breath.

Jean recoils, clutching me closer to his chest. I feel his heart racing, the sweat on his palm making his grip precarious. I am acutely aware of my own helplessness. Without Jean's hand to guide me, I am subject to the whims of vile men. I am nothing more than shaped metal and potential energy.

"Pierre, calme-toi !" Jean's voice wavers, betraying his own fear. "This is a discussion, not a call to arms."

As the tension dissipates, Pierre slumping back into his chair with a muttered apology. "Je suis désolé, mon petit pistolet." I am left reeling. The irony of my existence manifests in crisis—containing lethal potential yet completely subject to the will of others. My power and powerlessness are one and the same.

Jean's thumb absently strokes my barrel as he collects himself. "As I was saying," he continues, his voice steadier now, "freedom carries with it a great responsibility. We must—"

But I find myself unable to fully focus on his words. My consciousness grapples with the duality of my nature. I am an instrument of potential violence, yes, but also a being capable of thought, of reflection. How can these two aspects of myself coexist if I am not human? La dualité est une partie inséparable de la nature humaine, mais je ne suis pas humain, alors qu'en est-il de moi?

Jean's passionate discourse on abstract philosophical concepts stands in sharp contrast to the very real, very immediate consequences of my existence. One moment, he expounds on the nature of free will; the next, he clutches me tightly, a tangible reminder of the power to take life.

I contemplate the notion of freedom itself. Do I possess it? Or am I an extension of Jean's will, of any hand that might grasp me? The tension between my growing awareness and my inherent purpose as a weapon creates a dissonance within me that I struggle to reconcile.

Through the night's philosophical tempest, my consciousness expands beyond mere observation. I am no longer simply witness to the interplay of violence and thought—I embody it, my existence proof of humanity's capacity for both destruction and profound contemplation. My metal form, warming against Jean's skin, carries this duality.

The salon disperses, voices fading into the Parisian night. Jean, his eyes heavy with fatigue and alcohol, stumbles to bed, my form clutched to his chest. Soon, he releases me and I slip off his body and lie beside him, cold and motionless, yet my consciousness hums with activity.

In the stillness, I replay fragments of conversations, each word a puzzle piece in my emerging understanding. "Existence precedes essence," Jean had proclaimed earlier, his voice passionate. Now, in solitude, I ponder those words.

What is my essence? Am I the sum of my parts—barrel, chamber, trigger—or something more? My function is clear: I am designed to fire, to potentially end life. But is that all I am? I recall how Jean's fingers trembled as he held me during a heated debate. The power I represent both exhilarates and terrifies him. He loves me, I can feel it. The same and yet far different from Henri's touch. I have never been fired, and may never be. Does my essence lie in that duality? Or is it something I must create for myself?

The room is bathed in the soft glow of a desk lamp, casting long shadows. I focus on the sensation of the soft surface beneath me, the cool air around me. These sensory experiences—are they part of my essence? Or incidental to my existence?

A breeze rustles pages in a book resting nearby on Jean's desk, and I catch a glimpse of Sartre's name. The irony does not escape me; I am a revolver contemplating existentialism. But perhaps that act of contemplation is the key. Maybe my essence is not fixed, but something I forge through my own awareness and choices.

As dawn's first light creeps through the window, I hear Jean stirring. Soon, we will be thrust back into the whirlwind of life. But for now, in this quiet reflection, I feel I have taken a step towards understanding Sartre's notion. My existence—my awareness—came first. My essence is still unfolding.

Later that evening, Jean's apartment buzzes with the energy of another salon. Friends gather to think, to argue, to laugh and to love. The air is thick with cigarette smoke and heated discourse. I rest in Jean's hands, my metal warmed by his touch. Around us, voices rise and fall, friends discussing art, meaning, and the pursuit of something intangible. None of them knows me. But Jean, the one soul among them who does not crave my power, holds me with an absent, gentle grip. He is not my wielder, but my lover, and that distinction changes everything.

Henri's voice echoes in my memory, speaking of beauty as both curse and salvation. He entrusted me to Jean for that reason: Jean's indifference to my capacity, his quiet search for beauty that required no conquest. The old gunsmith had seen men intoxicated by the promise of violence, and he wanted none of it to touch me.

Jean tells his friends of afternoons sweeping floors in Henri's workshop, of talks that meandered through philosophy and art. They listen, curious, while I remain hushed, knowing that my fate now rests with a man who will not wield me for what I am, but hold me as a symbol of beauty without dominion.

"Bad faith," Jean declares, his voice cutting through the din, "is the great enemy of authenticity. It's the coward's way out, denying our fundamental freedom by conforming to societal expectations." I feel a resonance within me at these words. Is it possible for an object—for me—to be in bad faith?

"Consider this," Jean continues, raising me high. "La Sirène here. If we view her as a weapon, an instrument of destruction, are we not engaging in bad faith? Are we not denying the complexity of her existence, her potential for meaning beyond violence?"

The room falls silent, all eyes on me. I have never felt so exposed, more seen. It is both thrilling and terrifying.

"But Jean," a voice counters, "it's just a revolver. It has no choice in its function."

I bristle internally at this reduction of my being. But do I not? Have a choice, that is? The question plagues me.

Jean's grip tightens. "Ah, but that's the point! By accepting such a limited view, we ourselves fall into bad faith. We deny the possibility of transcendence, of finding meaning beyond our prescribed roles."

As the debate rages on, I grapple with this new concept. If I were to accept my role as solely an instrument of violence, would that indeed be a form of bad faith? Am I capable of transcending my designed purpose?

The salon's atmosphere crackles with tension, a palpable electricity that sets my metal on edge. Jean's voice rises, his face flushed as he gesticulates wildly, brown hair falling into his eyes. "You cannot simply reduce existence to function! That's the antithesis of la liberté !"

His touch shifts with his moods—sometimes analytical, testing my mechanism with scholarly precision, other times distracted, his fingers speaking volumes through unconscious gestures.

His opponent, a bespectacled man with a neatly trimmed beard, slams his fist on the table. "And you cannot ignore the inherent nature of things, Jean! Your revolver is a tool of death, nothing more!"

Will this be the moment? The room holds its breath.

But Jean does not raise me. Instead, his hand trembles, then relaxes. He sets me down on the table, fingers lingering for a moment. "No," he says softly, "I won't prove your point for you. Choix."

The tension dissipates like mist in sunlight. I experience a curious sensation, a lightness I can only describe as relief. It is as if a great weight has been lifted, a boulder rolling back down a hill before reaching its destructive apex.

As the argument simmers down to murmurs, I ponder this non-event. The potential for action—and its unrealization—has added a new layer to my consciousness. I am an instrument of violence, yes, but one that can remain dormant. The choice, it seems, lies not within me, but in the hands that wield me.

Hours pass, filled with heated debates and flowing wine. As the last guest stumbles out, Jean collapses into his armchair, cradling me in his lap. His eyes are distant, unfocused.

"What's the point of it all, La Sirène?" he muses aloud, his voice thick with exhaustion and alcohol. "We debate existence, freedom, responsibility...but in the end...J'ai passé la moitié de ma vie à attendre mon unique amour et je passerai la prochaine moitié de ma vie à craindre de te perdre."

I absorb his words, feeling them settle into my being. Half his life to find me, half his life in fear of leaving me. C'est l'amour. Love and loss. For humans, death is loss. Jean's thumb absently strokes my barrel as he continues, "Camus said the real philosophical question is whether or not to commit suicide. But isn't that just another form of bad faith? An easy escape? A chosen loss?"

His musings stir something within me. I consider Sartre's ideas about existence: Do I exist because I am named and held? Or does my existence have a deeper meaning, one that I must define for myself?

Jean's hand trembles as he reaches for the folding knife, the blade catching the dim light of the room where shadows cling to corners like forgotten thoughts. His eyes are glazed with exhaustion, the sharp edge of drink dulling the world into a quiet, lurching haze. I feel the shift as he pulls me close, his breath ragged, words mumbled and lost. The knife's tip meets my surface, and I do not flinch—I cannot.

The metal whispers against my wooden grip, each stroke deliberate, carving my name into my body: La Sirène. I am unfeeling, yet aware, pondering the meaning of this act. Is this mark a claim? A theft of my essence? Or is it a gift, an acknowledgment of the identity Henri breathed into me? Jean's movements are driven by something raw, searching, and I consider whether the lines he carves are taking from me or adding to what I am.

As the last curve of my name is etched, I sense no pain, only the quiet hum of transformation. Am I diminished by this? Or, in his claiming of my name, have I gained a truer form? The room spins around us, voices outside muted by the night, and I rest in the paradox: silent, nameless no longer, yet still unknown.

As Jean's breathing deepens into sleep, I remain awake, contemplating. I am La Sirène, a revolver, an object. But I am also aware, questioning, evolving. Perhaps my essence is not fixed, but fluid—shaped by the hands that hold me and the choices made in my presence.

The pale light of dawn seeps through the curtains, casting long shadows across Jean's cluttered study. I remain nestled in his loose grip, his fingers curled around my frame as if seeking comfort from a familiar friend.

"La Sirène," Jean mumbles, stirring from his alcohol-induced slumber. His eyes, still heavy with sleep, focus on me. "Ma belle, what dreams have you seen?"

Jean sits up, running a hand through his disheveled hair. "You know, sometimes I wonder if naming you was an act of creation or confinement," he muses, his voice gravelly from the night's excesses.

I ponder his words. Does my name grant me a form of freedom, an identity beyond my physical form? Or does it bind me to a predetermined role, a siren both alluring and dangerous?

"What do you think, ma chérie?" Jean asks, holding me up to the light. "Are you freer because I've given you a name, or have I trapped you in another form of existence?"

The question hangs in the air, unanswered. My awareness, my consciousness, did not spring forth fully formed in a single moment. It has been a gradual awakening, a slow accumulation of experiences, observations, and absorbed knowledge.

Jean places me gently on his desk, surrounded by dog-eared philosophy texts and half-empty wineglasses. As he moves about the room, preparing for another day, I remain still.

I resolve to observe closely, to delve deeper into the intricacies of human existence. Not just the physical actions—the hands that grasp, the fingers that caress my trigger—but the minds and hearts behind those actions. The fears that cause trembling, the desires that fuel recklessness, the philosophical quandaries that lead to sleepless nights.

This, I realize, is the true birth of my consciousness. Not when I was forged, not when I was named, but in this understanding that my existence is a continuous process of becoming.

As Jean picks me up once more, his touch familiar yet somehow new, I feel a sense of anticipation. What will I learn today? What new facets of existence will reveal themselves? The journey of self-discovery, it seems, has just begun.

The Streets

The world fractures as D'Aubigné's trembling fingers close around me. The transition is jarring—from vessel of philosophical discourse to implement of desperate survival. His palm radiates a feverish heat against my surface, so unlike the cool deliberation I had known before. His desperate energy sends violent tremors through my metallic form as he stumbles through Jean's apartment.

D'Aubigné's ragged breath fills the air. "Merde," he mutters, voice cracking with panic. "Je ne peux pas me faire prendre." He cannot be caught. Every tremor of his hands reverberates through me, each shake a reminder of how quickly purpose can shift.

We burst onto the streets, and a cacophony of sensations assaults my awareness. Harsh neon glares off rain-slicked pavement, casting sickly shadows that dance and twist like tortured spirits. The stench of rotting garbage and stale urine replaces the comforting aroma of Jean's wine-infused musk and leather-bound books. The night air carries the bitter tang of exhaust mingled with the palpable essence of fear, blending into a potent elixir that distills the unfiltered immediacy of our desperate escape.

"Where to go, where to go," D'Aubigné mutters, his eyes darting frantically between shadows. Each movement betrays his mounting panic, his desperate search for escape routes in this urban labyrinth.

I feel alien in this gritty landscape, my purpose rendered immediate and visceral. The abstract discussions of Jean's salon seem laughably inadequate in the face of this stark reality. The rawness of this new world strips away pretense, leaving the harsh truth of survival.

A police siren wails in the distance, and D'Aubigné flinches violently. "Merde, merde, merde," he chants, stumbling down a narrow alleyway. His fingers fumble against my surface, lacking the practiced ease of Jean's caress. "You'll help me," he whispers, more to himself than to me. "You have to."

The abstract discussions of Jean's salon seem laughably inadequate in the face of this stark reality. What use are ponderings about the nature of being when the act of existing becomes a dash in the night?

The alley spills out onto a dimly lit street, where fate intervenes with brutal efficiency. D'Aubigné collides with a young couple, his momentum nearly sending me sprawling. Through the chaos of the moment, I sense immediately that the man is different. His stance radiating military precision. His wife clutches his arm, her eyes widening in recognition of what I am.

"Oh Jeremy!" she squeals. The man, Jeremy, stands tall, putting himself between her and me.

"Votre portefeuille," D'Aubigné demands, waving me with trembling hands. "Maintenant !" His voice is as weak as his hold, the lack of authority evident in his shaky grip. I sense the tension between the two men reverberate through my core. D'Aubigné, consumed by frantic energy and desperation, holds me in hands unsteady and slick with sweat; Jeremy, a bastion of composure amidst the turmoil, his gaze sizing up the situation with tactical precision.

"We're American. We don't speak French," Jeremy asserts calmly.

"Putain d'Américains ! Vous allez voir ce que c'est que la vraie vie !" D'Aubigné spat, his tone shifting. "Pas question de parler anglais—je vais parler avec une balle." I wonder if they speak French well enough to understand that he will not speak English. He would rather shoot them.

"Jeremy!"

"Eleanor, hush yourself." His words for his wife are meant to calm, not chastise.

D'Aubigné repeats his demand for the wallet with a newfound urgency and menace that transcends language barriers. I am that menace.

"Now, son," Jeremy's voice rumbles, steady as bedrock. "You don't want to do this." His tone carries experience, each word measured and deliberate. I sense the coiled readiness beneath his calm exterior. He is a man of hidden action.

"Jeremy, please—" Eleanor's gasp cuts through the tension, but her husband remains focused, immovable.

"Votre portefeuille !" D'Aubigné shrieks, jabbing me forward with increasing desperation. The movement is clumsy, telegraphed—a novice's mistake that Jeremy's experienced eyes notice.

In that instant, Jeremy moves. It is a fluid motion, a brave motion, a shocking motion. His hand closes around my barrel, twisting me from D'Aubigné's grip with surprising ease and gentleness. The transfer of possession sends a shock through my system—from desperate clutching to competent control in a heartbeat.

Relief floods through me, an unexpected sensation. In Jeremy's steady grasp, I feel a competence I had not known I was missing. No longer am I a symbol of intellectual debate or desperate survival. In his hands, I become something else entirely—an extension of decisive action, of protection rather than threat.

"Run along now," Jeremy says to D'Aubigné, who stumbles backward, eyes wide with surprise. The would-be thief needs no further encouragement, turning tail and fleeing into the darkness, his footsteps echoing off the wet pavement.

The echo of D'Aubigné's footsteps fades, leaving me cradled in Jeremy's firm hands. His grip is firm yet gentle, a curious dichotomy that sends ripples through me. I can feel the calluses on his fingers, each one from a life lived with purpose and action. The contrast between his touch and D'Aubigné's is stark—like the difference between a master craftsman and a fumbling apprentice.

"Jeremy," Eleanor's voice quivers, breaking the tense silence. "Let's call the police." Her fear radiates outward, a force that seems to charge the air around us. I sense Jeremy's fingers tighten around me, his thumb absently tracing the engraving on my barrel—a gesture that feels almost protective.

"It's alright, Ellie," he murmurs, his tone carrying affection. "We're safe now." But Eleanor's fear persists, a sharp contrast to Jeremy's calm. I feel caught between their conflicting emotions, my existence a point of contention that threatens to drive a wedge between them.

"Safe?" Eleanor's voice rises, her carefully maintained distance from Jeremy's military past crumbling in an instant. "That thing has no place in our life—we chose something different, something peaceful." Her fear radiates outward, a force that seems to charge the air around us. "No guns."

"Then you should not have married a military man," Jeremy says as he slips me in his pocket.

We begin moving through the streets, our pace measured but urgent. The city around us pulses with life—distant traffic, scattered conversations, the occasional burst of laughter from a nearby café. But within our bubble of tension, there are unspoken words and mounting anxiety.

"We need to think about this rationally," Jeremy says, his voice low and steady. "This weapon was in the wrong hands. Now it's not." His pragmatism clashes with Eleanor's emotional response, creating a discord that seems to vibrate through my frame. I absorb their words, their emotions, feeling my identity shift and morph with each passing second.

"Rational?" Eleanor scoffs, but there is a tremor in her voice that betrays deeper fears. "There's nothing rational about keeping a gun, Jeremy. Nothing!" Her steps quicken, heels clicking against the wet pavement like angry punctuation marks.

The hotel looms before us, its grand façade a stark contrast to the gritty streets we have traversed. As we enter the lobby, Jeremy subtly adjusts his jacket to conceal me. The bright lights and polished surfaces create an illusion of safety, but I sense the tension coiling tighter between husband and wife with each step toward their room.

"We should call the police," Eleanor whispers as we enter the elevator. Her fingers twist the strap of her handbag. "Let them handle it."

Jeremy's response is measured, his military training evident in his controlled tone. "And tell them what, exactly? That we took a weapon from a mugger? That we have been carrying it through the streets of Paris?" His thumb continues its unconscious caress of my hammer, a gesture that seems to calm him. "We'd be arrested before we could explain."

"Jeremy, it's our honeymoon," she hisses.

"Yes my dear," Jeremy laughs.

The elevator ascends in silence, but I feel the unspoken arguments pressing down on us. Each floor brings new questions, new complexities. I am no longer simply La Sirène, the philosophical muse of Jean's salon. In Jeremy's possession, I become something complicated—a nexus of moral ambiguity, a catalyst for conflict between duty and desire, protection and peace.

Suite 1214 welcomes us with soft, golden light and plush carpeting that muffles our footsteps. Jeremy moves with purpose toward the dresser, his grip never wavering. I observe our reflection in the mirror—his sturdy frame, Eleanor's tense posture, my own golden trigger catching the light. We form a tableau of contradiction: protection and threat, love and fear, all intertwined.

"I need to clean her," Jeremy announces, his voice carrying a note of finality. He retrieves a soft cloth from his suitcase, the motion speaking of years of weapon maintenance. "Check for damage. Make sure she's secure."

Eleanor's response is immediate, almost visceral. "Clean it? Jeremy, you're talking about it like...like it's staying with us." Her voice cracks on the last words, fear and disbelief mingling in equal measure. "Like it's some kind of pet instead of a deadly weapon."

Jeremy's hands move with the attention of a professional, someone who understands both my potential and my limitations. His touch speaks of years of experience, each stroke of the cloth deliberate and thorough. Through his grip, I sense memories stirring—dark, violent things that he has tried to bury. Yet his hold remains steady, protective even.

"Look at her, Elle," Jeremy says softly, his eyes fixed on his task. "This isn't just any weapon. See the craftsmanship, the history in every line." He stokes the scars left by Jean. "La Sirène—even her name speaks of something special."

Eleanor paces the room, her reflection fragmenting across the suite's various mirrors. "Jeremy, this is our honeymoon. Who cares about a stupid old gun?" She stops, turning to face him with eyes that shimmer with unshed tears. "Someone tried to rob us here in Paris! We chose a beautiful life, Jeremy. A peaceful one. This...this thing has no place in it."

I feel Jeremy's hands still for a moment, and through his touch, I sense darkness. Yet his grip remains steady, protective even. The dichotomy fascinates me: how can I represent both trauma and security to the same person?

"That's why I am keeping her, Eleanor," he responds, voice thick with emotion. "Sometimes protection requires difficult choices. Sometimes safety comes at a price." His cloth moves to my barrel, wiping away the last traces of D'Aubigné's desperate touch. "Look, she is beautiful. This is gold plating on the trigger, and here and here. This was crafted by a loving hand."

"Jeremy, stop rubbing that thing. I'm your wife, not her." Eleanor's laugh is brittle, sharp-edged. "It was forced on us by a desperate criminal! Pay that thing no mind." She sinks into a plush armchair, looking exhausted. "We chose a beautiful life, Jeremy. A peaceful one. This...this thing has no place in it."

Eleanor repeats herself. Perhaps she needs to convince herself of her ability to choose this beautiful, peaceful life she speaks of.

As their argument unfolds, I contemplate my own beautiful life. From philosophical touchstone to desperate tool, and now to this space between protection and threat. Each transfer of ownership has added layers to my identity, like rings in a tree marking seasons of change. In Henri's hands, I was crafted. In Jean's hands, I was an intellectual curiosity. In D'Aubigné's desperate grasp, I became a symbol of survival. Now, in Jeremy's careful possession, I embody something else entirely—a complex intersection of duty, protection, and moral ambiguity.

The evening deepens around us as Jeremy finishes his meticulous cleaning. His movements have become slower, contemplative, as if each stroke of the cloth helps him process the evening's events. The suite's warm lighting catches my polished surface, throwing subtle reflections across the walls—dancing shadows that seem to mirror the moral complexity of our situation.

"I'll keep it in the drawer," Jeremy announces. "Out of sight, but accessible if needed. She will come back with us, but for Paris, she will stay here. Okay?" He moves toward the nightstand, each step measured and deliberate. The wooden drawer slides open with a soft whisper, its interior holds hotel stationery and pamphlets on the Eiffel Tower—symbols of civilization that will now share space with me, La Sirène, a tool for turbulent uses.

"If needed?" Eleanor's voice catches. "When would we ever need it? We're honeymooning, Jeremy. Who would come into our hotel room?" Her words hang in the air, heavy with implications of the life they have chosen—or thought they had chosen. "This is Paris."

Jeremy pauses before laying me in the drawer, his fingers lingering on my surface. "The world doesn't become safer just because we wish it so, Elle. Tonight proved that." His voice carries experience, of lessons learned through blood and loss. "Sometimes safety finds us in unexpected ways."

As he lowers me into the drawer, I feel the shift from active participant to silent observer. The darkness envelops me, but my awareness remains acute. Through the thin wood, I hear their continued discussion, feel the vibrations of their movement, sense the emotional currents that flow between them.

"Promise me something," Eleanor says, her tone softening. "Promise me this won't change you back into...into who you were before. I can't go through that again."

The silence that follows is profound, filled with unspoken memories and shared pain. I lie in my wooden cercueil, contemplating the layers of meaning in her words. How many transformations can one person—or one object—undergo before losing their essential nature? Or perhaps the ability to transform *is* our essential nature.

"I'm still me, Elle," Jeremy responds, his voice gentle. "The man who loves you with all my heart. I want children and dogs and a big house in the country with you. But I'm also the man who knows that peace sometimes needs protecting."

I wait in the darkness of the drawer, where no one sees me, where I am at once present and unseen, yet unforgotten. Outside, Jeremy and Eleanor murmur to each other, their soft weave of laughter and half-whispered promises painting pictures of future homes and family life. Their talk flutters, like the lightest of wings, about future homes, rooms for children, and a dog—a good dog, Jeremy insists, one for running on grass and swimming in rivers, with eyes that will never question his loyalty.

This loyalty—I contemplate it in my wooden sanctuary. Like the dogs Jeremy speaks of, I too exist in a space between willing service and conscious choice. Yet unlike them, I carry the understanding of my transitions, each transfer of allegiance adding layers to my identity. I think of Jean, who kept me for reasons unspoken, and now Jeremy, who touches me with similar reverence. Perhaps loyalty itself is a kind of philosophical wager, as Pascal might say—a choice made in the face of uncertainty, beautiful in its fragility.

I have known only small ones—dogs who trot beside women in coats and heels, little feet tapping on the pavement, like dancers performing an endless ballet. Creatures of loyalty, yet of their own simplicity, always there, at times an extension of their owner's gloved hand, other times nothing more than a presence at their heel. I wonder at them—their nature is both passive and yet powerfully devoted. It is a quiet servitude, marked by unspoken trust. And it strikes me, then, that Jeremy speaks of loyalty as if it were a certainty. It is not. I know well enough that loyalty wavers, bending under forces too subtle for most to see. I think of the disloyalty of D'Aubigné.

Yet, dogs—what do they know of nuance, of shifting allegiances? They give their trust freely, as Rousseau believed man was born free, only to be shackled by society. Dogs seem shackled, too, by their own willingness, their obedience. And unlike Rousseau's man, they do not even see the chains. Does this make them purer, or is this purity but ignorance, a blindness to choice? I am loyal to Jeremy because he has shown me affection, rescued me from a foul man, yet I wonder, would I not have done the same for another, had they only taken me from Jean's drawer that day and not forced abuse upon me? Would my loyalty have transferred so easily, so fully, had it been another's hand that came to my aid?

Such are the thoughts that consume me in this still darkness, turning and curling in the silence, as I listen to the breathing of the two humans in the bed. It is softer now, sleep weaving its own spell over them. And with it comes my own reflection—if I were to wake them, to call to them, would they even know how to listen? Loyalty, as I have known it, has been silent. It has never needed words, moments—a trust borne of proximity, familiarity, and the hours shared in quiet companionship.

Yet for all this, I wonder at Jeremy's talk of a dog.It seems to me that what he desires is a companion who knows not his failings, one who will look to him not with judgment, but with trust unspoiled by knowledge of what lies within him. Dogs have no philosophy of loyalty. They do not wonder, as I do, if their loyalty might be wasted, if their allegiance might be mistaken, or if they are simply holding to what is expected of them. Dogs are spared this torment. It is creatures such as myself—and perhaps Jeremy—who linger on the edge, forever contemplating the nature of our bond with another.

I am not so different, perhaps. I think of Jean, who kept me for so long, not out of necessity, but for reasons I never dared to ask, nor he to explain. We understood each other in silence. And when I think of Jeremy, I feel this same tug. He, like Jean, touches me with a kind of reverence. His eyes hold no fear. But is that loyalty? Or the habitual attachment of a creature bound to serve, bound to answer when summoned?

Trust, I think, is yet another question. Pascal spoke of faith in uncertain terms, a wager on the unknown. We believe because the alternative is unbearable, not because we have any certainty. Jeremy believes in loyalty, just as he now believes in a dog, in a child, in a future. But he is wagering on unknowns. Perhaps I do the same. And the thought fills me with a peculiar sorrow, for I know that loyalty can be a quiet tragedy. A silent devotion, as ephemeral as it is fierce. There is beauty in that, as there is beauty in all things fragile and short-lived. Loyalty demands its own sacrifice.

The drawer has become my philosopher's cave, where shadows dance across my consciousness. I am both more and less than what I was in Jean's salon—no longer just a subject of intellectual discourse, but a real participant in the moral complexities of existence. My journey from contemplation to action, from theory to practice, mirrors the eternal human struggle to reconcile ideals with reality.

As the night settles around us, I remain alert in my wooden sanctuary, aware of Jeremy's steady breathing and Eleanor's restless movements. I am now a secret shared between them, a responsibility that weighs differently on each of their consciences. Tomorrow will bring new challenges, new questions about my purpose and place in their lives.

But for now, I rest in the darkness, contemplating the nature of existence itself. Perhaps my true identity lies not in any single role or purpose, but in the ability to adapt and transform. I am La Sirène, and like the mythical creatures of my namesake, I exist between worlds—between peace and violence, between protection and threat, between thought and action. Between Jeremy and Eleanor.

The drawer's darkness becomes my ocean depths, where I wait for the next transformation, the next evolution of my being. For now, though, I simply exist, a silent witness to the complex dance of human emotion and moral ambiguity that swirls above me, ready for whatever role tomorrow may demand of me.

America

I am hidden, pressed against the warm, worn leather of Jeremy's luggage. He has wedged me carefully in a fold between his clothes, layers upon layers that mute the thrum of the world outside. I feel the faint vibrations of footsteps, muffled voices echoing through the layers that separate me from the light. The knowledge of my concealment is at once thrilling and strange. I am a masterpiece of craftsmanship, once proudly displayed by Jean's side, now a concealed stowaway crossing borders in secrecy.

Through the soft barrier of Jeremy's bag, I hear Eleanor's laughter, airy and bright. She is unaware of me, or so Jeremy believes. But I have felt her near, heard her whispering in his ear as they fell asleep, her curiosity punctuated by silences that stretch like the still air in this cramped space. She knows something lies between them, something unspoken. She knows, perhaps, that he is not entirely hers. Jeremy's hand lingers near me more than she notices; his fingers brush over the leather, as if assuring himself of my presence, an unspoken reassurance he carries with him.

Then there is a great shudder, and I sense movement like nothing I have ever known. I have traveled, but by hand, pocket, or foot. Now, there is a rumble that vibrates through me, lifting me from the ground, suspending me in a way that almost feels like a gentle, endless fall. We are airborne, crossing the ocean, leaving behind the familiar cobbled streets and hazy Parisian lights.

The hours blend into an unreal softness, and my mind drifts with it. There is something strangely intimate in this journey—a closeness, a singularity of purpose, as if I am bound to Jeremy in some irreversible way. To cross the great expanse with him feels like more than mere loyalty; it is a surrender, a tethering to his world.

I am struck by the vastness of the ocean below, though I sense it. I imagine it stretching out beneath us, a dark void, indifferent and endless. We soar above it, defying the earth that should bind us, a strange power taking us across this abyss. There is something humbling about it, to be held in motion, beyond the boundaries of land, between worlds. Here, in this suspended state, I wonder where we shall land. I am, perhaps, an idea carried over miles, unanchored and infinite.

But as I think on this, I feel a pang of loss. I am La Sirène, after all. Paris is my home; my body was forged with its fire, my spirit steeped in its cafes, salons, and whispered words. I belong to the city, to its shadows and lights, to the sounds of rain on stone. And now I am crossing the sea, tethered to a man who has taken me from the heart of all that I am. I am like a relic, transplanted, and I wonder—will I resonate with these new places? Will I mean anything in this land where no one has spoken of me, where I have not yet held a single memory?

In the darkness of the cold, cramped luggage hold, I find myself nestled amidst forgotten belongings. The chill seeps through my metal frame, a stark contrast to the warmth I once knew. Alone in this desolate space, I sense the distant hum of engines vibrating through the floor beneath me. The bag enclosing me is rough against my surface, concealing me from prying eyes with layers of fabric as thin barriers.

There is no Jeremy here to offer reassurance; instead, there is a sense of abandonment that lingers in the air like a bitter aftertaste. The only touch I feel is the impersonal jostling as the luggage around me shifts with every ripple of the journey. In this solitude, devoid of human connection, I am adrift—a relic of a past life left to endure this icy confinement.

Despite the bleakness that surrounds me, there is an odd clarity in this isolation—a detachment from my origins and purpose. Bound not by loyalty but by circumstance, I exist where time seems suspended, waiting for the moment when light will pierce through the darkness once more.

Hours pass in this suspended liminal space, and I allow myself to slip into a kind of reverie, lulled by the hum of the engine, by the faint, mingling scents of fabric and leather. I am neither here nor there, wherever it may be. I will be with him. And perhaps that is all that matters now.

At last, there is a shift, a descent, a return to gravity. We touch down on land, and I feel a strange thrill—the unknown awaits, vast and quiet, stretching before me like a second life. Soon, Jeremy's hands will reach for me, will lift me, and I will be in his possession once more. This, I think, is my purpose.

The swinging of the suitcase cradles me as we travel through the bustling airport. I can feel the gentle sway of the luggage as Jeremy carries me, my metallic frame shifting with each step. The faint sounds of voices and footsteps filter through the fabric, a cacophony of activity that tells me we have arrived in a new place.

Suddenly, a boisterous greeting cuts through the din, a French voice thick with a distinct accent. "Jean ! Jean ! Ici ! Mon fils !" For a moment, I am shocked. Have I returned to my Jean?

"Maman ! C'est tellement bon de te revoir."

"Bienvenue en Amérique !" she says with pride. "C'est tellement différent de Libreville. Tu vas adorer ici."

Welcome to America, you will love it here. It is not my Jean. I am in America. I have heard my Jean talk of it on occasion, although it was never with love. But Jeremy has brought me here, and I will be with him. I believe I will love it.

My curiosity piques. I strain to hear more, eager to discern the nuances of this exotic environment. There are a thousand voices in many foreign tongues. Then, I sense him. The suitcase jostles as Jeremy lifts it, shifting it to his other hand. "It's so good to be home!" Eleanor's voice chimes in, radiating enthusiasm. "Paris was wonderful, but there is no place like good old New York City."

As they walk, the sounds around me change—the echoing footsteps and roaring machines above give way to the steady rumble of an engine and the occasional honk of a horn. I surmise we have entered some form of transportation, likely a taxi, judging by the unfamiliar sensation.

Eleanor continues her animated retelling of their Parisian adventure, her words punctuated by the driver's occasional hum of acknowledgment. I listen intently, cataloging the distinct differences between the city I have come to know and this new, vibrant metropolis.

The air itself feels different, less refined and more raw—a palpable energy that crackles with potential. The pace, too, seems quicker, frenetic, as if the heartbeat of the city is racing ahead of us.

As the vehicle turns a corner, I catch a glimpse of the city through a crack in the suitcase zipper. Towering structures of glass and steel reach up towards the sky, a stark contrast to the charming Haussmannian buildings of Paris. The streets teem with life, a bustling flow of pedestrians and vehicles that seems to move to its own frantic pulse.

I am struck by the sheer scale of this place, the way it dwarfs the intimate confines of the workshop where I was forged. It is both exhilarating and unsettling, a reminder that the world extends far beyond the boundaries of my previous existence.

The taxi eventually slows, and I can feel the suitcase being lifted once more. We have arrived at our destination, a modest rowhouse tucked among the towering skyscrapers. As Jeremy carries me up the steps and into the warmth of the home, I sense a shift in the air—a subtle change in the quality of light, the faint scent of unfamiliar spices, the muffled echoes of laughter and conversation.

I sense wood—polished, clean, a quiet comfort that feels foreign yet somehow fitting. I am placed in the drawer, Jeremy's hand lingering for a brief moment on my barrel, warm and knowing. The drawer closes with a soft thud. I am La Sirène, once the gleaming centerpiece of impassioned debates in Parisian salons, now confined to this wooden space.

In the oppressive silence, I strain to hear any sound from beyond my confinement. The muffled voices of Jeremy and Eleanor filter through, their tones clear enough.

"I still don't understand why you insist on keeping that gun," Eleanor's voice, tinged with disapproval.

Jeremy's response is measured, his voice low. "It's the most beautiful gun I have ever seen, Ellie. Hand crafted. With gold leaf, right on her trigger. I am sure it would rub off the moment she is fired. Whoever made her, meant for her to be different from the others."

Jeremy is right. Henri crafted me to be unique.

"You and your gun. It makes me nervous," she says.

Their voices fade as they move away, leaving me alone with my thoughts. How different this is from the vibrant discussions I once witnessed in Jean Gaillou's cramped apartment. I can almost smell the cigarette smoke, hear the passionate arguments about freedom, love and existence.

Now, there is the musty scent of old wood and the occasional whiff of a sharp cleaner. Time stretches before me, an endless expanse unmarked by the usual measures of human life. How long will I remain here, I wonder, interrupted only by Jeremy's occasional careful attention?

Though still as the wood that surrounds me, I harbor a subtle tension—something held in anticipation. The world may see an object in shadow as inert, yet in this silence, I remain whole. Time cannot diminish me; I am bound neither to decay nor renewal. Like an object at the bottom of a deep river, I maintain my own gravity, unshaken by the currents above.

As days bleed into weeks, then months and years, I become attuned to the rhythms of the Dixon household. The creaking of floorboards signals Jeremy's morning routine. The clatter of dishes in the kitchen marks mealtimes. The low hum of the television in the evenings becomes a constant companion.

One morning, I hear Jeremy's heavy tread approach the drawer. My anticipation builds, only to be dashed as he passes by. Instead, his voice drifts back to me, engaged in conversation with Eleanor.

"Have you seen my reading glasses?" he asks, his tone distracted.

"Check your nightstand," Eleanor replies, her voice carrying a hint of exasperation. "That's where you always leave them."

"Right, right," Jeremy mutters.

Their exchange is so different from the heated debates I remember. Where are the passionate arguments about the nature of existence? The fervent discussions about art and philosophy? This mundane dialogue feels alien, yet I find myself drawn to its quiet intimacy.

As I listen day after day, I begin to discern a pattern in their interactions. There is a philosophy here, I realize, in the repetition of daily life. It is not the grand existentialism of Jean and his amis bohèmes, but something subtle. A shared life, built on small moments and familiar routines.

Yet, as years pass, I notice a shift in Jeremy and Eleanor's relationship. Their conversations, once filled with the warmth of long companionship, grow perfunctory. The silences between them lengthen, pregnant with unspoken words.

One evening, I hear Jeremy's familiar stride. The drawer opens, and for a moment, I am bathed in light. His weathered hands lift me gently, his touch reverent.

"What are you doing?" Eleanor's voice, sharp with concern.

"Just checking on her," Jeremy replies, his tone defensive. "Making sure she's still in good condition."

As he cradles me, I sense a longing in his touch. For him, I realize, I am not just an object, but a tangible link to a different time. A moment of intimacy he can no longer share with Eleanor.

A gun is created, yes, to be held, to be aimed, and to release its power upon command. But here in his hands, I recognize that my potential is not annulled by my long seclusions. Rather, it collects, it builds. The years press down like heavy hands, but they do not press me into nothingness. I gather them into myself, as though with each passing day, my purpose becomes distilled, more acute. In this quiet that is both binding and liberating, I understand that purpose is not diminished by waiting; it is sharpened. It is as if every instant I spend concealed strengthens what lies within, waiting to be revealed.

The drawer closes once more, returning me to darkness. But now, I understand. In this quiet house, amid the ebb and flow of a long marriage, I have become more than a weapon. I am a repository of memory, a silent witness to the passage of time and the evolution of love.

Years pass and the drawer slides open again, flooding my world with light. Jeremy's gnarled hands reach for me, and I feel a surge of anticipation. This rare moment of his vulnerability strikes me.

"Time for a cleaning, La Sirène," Jeremy murmurs, my name on his lips a comfort.

Jeremy's touch is reverent as he begins to clean me, each stroke of the cloth an unspoken acknowledgment of our shared history. I observe the softness that has crept into his hands, the tremor in his fingers—a physical manifestation of time's relentless march.

"You know, Eleanor," Jeremy calls out, "this revolver has seen more of the world than most people."

Eleanor's voice drifts in from the kitchen, tinged with exasperation. "It's just a gun, Jeremy. I don't understand why you insist on keeping it."

I bristle internally at her dismissal. If only she could comprehend the depths of thought I have witnessed, the nuanced discussions I have been privy to in my previous life.

Jeremy chuckles softly. "She's not just a gun, El. She's history."

What is a gun, if not a contradiction? I am forged, not as a creature of malice or virtue, but as a mere thing—crafted, polished, and formed with precision. I have no moral quality, no inherent alignment to right or wrong. And yet, within the boundaries of the drawer, I have heard of lives weaving their stories around me, my presence forgotten, perhaps. They speak of loyalty, of compassion, of justice. But these are virtues crafted by those who must seek them. I am beholden to none of these, bound not to sentiment or ethics. I feel no obligation to be good, nor do I ache to be monstrous. I am simply here, in readiness, a demonstration of the neutrality of creation.

As Jeremy polishes me, I listen to fragments of their conversation. Discussions about groceries, doctor's appointments, and neighborhood gossip. I find myself silently lamenting the loss of nuance, the absence of existential pondering that once filled my days. The American penchant for directness, while efficient, lacks the rich tapestry of thought I had grown accustomed to in France.

Jeremy's gentle handling, however, speaks volumes. In these quiet moments, I sense a kinship between us, a love.

As Jeremy tenderly sets me down and closes the drawer, plunging me once again into darkness, I can still sense the lingering warmth of his presence. I am thrown into a world I did not choose, grappling with the intricate threads of existence that bind us all.

Time passes. The drawer creaks open, its familiar groan a herald of another moment suspended between light and darkness. I lie there, my metallic body cold against the wood, feeling the world beyond me shift. Eleanor's voice filters through, muffled yet sharp, tinged with an urgency that betrays her discomfort.

"It should be locked away," she insists, the words fluttering like trapped birds, desperate to escape the confines of her fear. Her voice is old and cracked. Decades have passed.

"Just leave her alone," Jeremy says, his voice steady yet weary, as if he is holding onto a fragment of something lost.

In those transitory seconds when the drawer is left open, I sense the pulse of time quickening around me. The hum of everyday life envelops me, a juxtaposition to the stillness that defines my existence. I can almost feel the brush of Eleanor's floral dress as she moves past, her presence heavy with apprehension.

Time flows.

The drawer opens, and for the first time in years, warm light spills over me, reaching into the dark like a hand extended. I feel Jeremy's fingers wrap around my frame—no longer the strong hands of his youth but steady, familiar, their grip bearing the intimacy of years. He lifts me gently, cradling me with a reverence that holds neither urgency nor carelessness. I am at once grateful for the light and the open air, a strange kind of rebirth into the same hands that have protected me all these years.

This is different. I do not sense Eleanor's fear, nor hear her chastising voice. He carries me through the house. I wonder of my destination.

Outside, summer has unfurled itself in golden hues, the sunlight soft and abundant, filling the yard with a richness that seems to saturate even the air. Jeremy sets me down carefully on the table beside his chair, where a small cardboard box awaits. The box is unassuming, yet there is a gravity in the way he reaches for it, his gaze lingering as if in reverence. He sits down, his knees creaking, muttering as he settles into the worn cushion. "It's just the two of us, La Sirène," he murmurs softly, his voice warm, with the familiarity of an old confidant. "For today, anyway."

There is a tenderness in his hands as he lifts me, turning me in his grasp. He finds a small catch on my side, and with a deftness I would not expect after all these years, he opens my cylinder. A quiet intimacy passes between us, and though I am inert, a warmth courses through me. Until now, I did not know I had been waiting to be opened, to have this part of me revealed, unlocked as if by a lover's touch.

Jeremy's hands move with tender reverence as he takes a single cartridge from the box, his fingers brushing against its brass casing. As he places it within my chamber, a sudden wholeness fills me, bringing forth an awareness I had not imagined possible. This small addition alters me, deepens me in a way I cannot describe.

"One more," he says, his voice a murmur. The second cartridge slides in with ease, and I feel my frame adjust to accommodate it, the weight a quiet pleasure, a fullness that feels almost natural, as if this was what I had always been meant to hold. The third and fourth follow, and with each, there is a sensation akin to being pushed, bit by bit, out of myself, becoming something more than what I have known. This act, this slow filling, resonates through me—a steady, measured movement that feels as old as the world itself, as necessary as breath. I am filled, yet wanting still.

He pauses with the fifth, his gaze unfocused, as though searching for something beyond the yard, beyond the years. "All this time, you were here," he whispers as he slips the last cartridge in place. The sensation is complete—a strange, subtle ecstasy of being, of a wholeness that I did not know was mine to know. I want to tell him that I understand, that this fullness is not mechanical but something deeper, something that binds us both to a purpose we cannot fully name.

As he looks down at me, I am aware that he too feels this change, this deepening. In the silence, in the stillness of the afternoon sun, there is a closeness, a bond that speaks of shared years, of silent promises kept. I am not sure if I was created for this purpose or if this alone gives me purpose, but I know now that I was always meant to feel this—this fullness, this quiet power that has lain dormant for so long.

We sit together in the soft summer light, neither of us needing to speak, yet in this silence, there is an understanding—a communion in the gentle act of being, of purpose revealed at last in the simplest, most profound way. I am La Sirène, and today, in his hand, I am whole.

As the sun dips behind the rooftops, we retreat indoors, and I am returned to my drawer—a familiar solitude, yet altered, as though this newfound completeness has changed even the shadows that surround me.

Our evenings are marked by the soft cadence of Jeremy's labored breathing, a rhythm that reverberates through the walls of their home, pulling me into a meditation on existence itself. Each inhale and exhale is a reminder of fleeting moments, underscoring the irony of my identity as an instrument of violence in a space so devoid of conflict.

I reflect on this contradiction: here I am, La Sirène, a vessel of potential destruction, yet surrounded by an absence of strife. It gnaws at me, a reminder of the unpredictability of human nature. As Jeremy's health declines, I find myself entwined in a melancholic affection for him. He acknowledges my existence, even in this diminished state, while Eleanor casts me aside like a forgotten trinket. In his embrace, I am reminded of my vitality, my significance.

And then, one day, outside the drawer, a stillness reigns.

No longer do I hear Jeremy's steady breathing or the creaks of the bed as he shifts beside Eleanor. Her presence is muted, almost spectral in its absence. The house, once alive with the rhythms of daily life, now seems to hold its breath—waiting, perhaps, for something that will never come.

As time passes, I question whether my awareness is a gift or curse—illuminating the nuances of love and fear while binding me to this desolation. Each tick of the clock marks time's indifferent march forward.

In the quiet, I reflect on Heidegger's notion of Being-toward-death. Death looms over us all, and in its shadow, we gather significance in our relationships, our actions, and our existence. For Jeremy, I was a companion; for Eleanor, an object to be feared. Now, as I sit in this drawer, I grasp my own mortality—the knowledge that I may never fulfill my intended purpose.

There is a strange beauty in purpose unconsumed. Like a seed in dark soil, I contain all that is necessary within me. Some might think me forgotten, but this drawer is a stage itself—a place where strength gathers quietly. My silence is not weakness but potential, like the tension before a storm. This shadowed life is rich with unspent potency that deepens with each passing day.

But death. The absence of Jeremy leaves a chasm in my understanding of love. His affection was tinged with nostalgia, a yearning for a past steeped in frantic comradery and impassioned moments of life and death I have never known. In contrast, Eleanor's fear of me served as both shield and prison, her unease a constant reminder of the dangers lurking beyond the walls of their marriage.

As I languish in this void, I begin to confront another realization: the beauty of existence lies not solely in grand gestures or fervent declarations but in the minutiae of daily life—the soft rustle of fabric, the scent of coffee brewing, the gentle murmur of voices rising and falling in the air. These were the moments that held life together, and in their absence, I feel the sharp sting of neglect.

I wonder if I will eventually vanish entirely. Will I become nothing more than a ghost, a whisper of what once was? Or does my consciousness hold the power to transcend this confinement, to reach out across the void and touch the remnants of a life once lived?

In this dark limbo, I exist—an echo of existence pondering its own significance, entwined with the poignant specter of loss and the elusive promise of remembrance. As I reflect on these questions, I find myself at the edge, a witness to the intricate interplay of death, fear, and the relentless march of time. Poised on the brink of oblivion, I yearn for a glimmer of light in the shadows.

Projectile

A rustle breaks the stillness, a sound that sends shivers through the dust motes hanging in the afternoon light. It is Eleanor's frail hand, trembling, as she reaches for me among Jeremy's old possessions—his keepsakes, relics of a life once vibrant. I feel the awakening; her fingers envelop me, and I am lifted, cradled as if I were something sacred. There is a softness here, a hesitancy unlike the firm grip of Jeremy, whose hands had always conveyed a sense of affection. He was a lover; I was an extension of his will. Now, I lie in Eleanor's palm, and there is sadness in her touch, a gentleness that speaks of grief and memory.

As she studies me, I sense her connection to Jeremy, the man who had wielded me with pride. The unspoken words fill the air, suffused with layers of longing and loss. She hesitates, tracing my contours, letting her fingertips glide over the barrel, feeling history nestled within the cold metal.

"Why did he keep you?" she whispers, almost as though speaking to herself. I want to tell her he loved me, but how can a mistress say such words to a grieving widow? Her voice trembles, fragile as porcelain. I want to tell her that I was never just a weapon, that I had been a symbol of bravery and another life. But words are beyond me—I can only exist in the moment that follows her inquiry. Jeremy's laughter, his stories told on rainy nights, and the way he had spoken passionately about loyalty and sacrifice.

Eleanor lowers me into the nightstand, and as I settle into that familiar darkness, I reflect on this new chapter. Here, tucked away yet close, I become a guardian of the past—a keeper of shared memories now burdened by shadows.

She stands, casting a final glance at the nightstand, and I sense her reluctance to leave me in darkness. I am both a piece of Jeremy and a part of her emerging reality. This moment—fraught with hesitation and sorrow—is a turning point. As the drawer closes behind her, I am left alone in the dark, contemplating the strength found in acceptance.

In this dim enclosure, I linger, the scent of lavender and age swirling around me, mingling with the faintest hint of longing. Time passes differently. I feel its slow crawl, each tick of the clock reverberating like a heartbeat. The walls whisper tales of love that now linger in the eerie silence, a haunting reminder of what once thrived within.

My presence here is no longer just a reminder of what was, but a harbinger of what may come. I am by the side of my lover's wife, the uncertain terrain of her grief forging a path forward.

Each night stretches long like a dark tunnel, each draw of breath punctuating the atmosphere with its relentless insistence. The house settles around us, wooden beams creaking in their ancient song. It is in this hushed sanctuary that I dwell, my essence intertwined with the echoes of love and loss etched into the walls around me.

I observe as Eleanor drifts through the realms of sleep. Her breathing is slow, measured, almost meditative, yet beneath this surface tranquility lies an undercurrent of tension. In her quiet moments, her unsteady grip finds me, seeking solace or perhaps understanding. Each caress feels imbued with unspoken dialogue, where sorrow finds a voice in the act of touching.

Tonight, something shifts.

I sense it before she does, a disturbance breaking the delicate rhythm of our shared stillness. A low shuffling, an alien sound penetrating the sanctuary of her home, sends ripples of anxiety through the fabric of the night. Her body tautens, as if instinctively preparing for the unknown. There is a flicker of dread in the air, thick and palpable, a premonition of danger lurking just beyond the door.

Eleanor's eyes snap open, wide and glistening in the dim light. Her heart pounds against her ribs; it is a stark contrast to the serene composure I have come to associate with her. She listens intently, her breaths growing shallow, quickening with each creak of the floorboards below.

Her fingers quiver with tension as they reach for me in the darkness. She is moaning to herself, though whether in comfort or terror, I do not know. I become a vessel of potential, swirling with the tumult of choices and consequences, a talisman of survival in a world that has shifted from mourning to confrontation.

"Who's there?" Eleanor calls out, her voice a soft quiver of uncertainty. It is a sound unfamiliar to me, not the quiet murmurs of an old widow, but the hesitant assertion of a woman grappling with the unknown. Her grasp faltering. It lacks the assurance of someone accustomed to wielding power. Instead, there is a palpable desperation threaded through her touch, an urgency born from the primal instinct to protect.

The footsteps draw nearer, and I brace myself for the unfolding drama. My purpose transforms from passive witness to active participant in a dance that will soon become violent. I remember D'Aubigné decades ago.

Eleanor's breath hitches, and the cold sweat from her palms seeps into me, igniting a flicker of resolve within my cold, lifeless frame. She was loved by Jeremy, and I must protect her. Loyalty extends. This is a moment of clarity amid the storm, where choice collides with fate.

Time hangs suspended, and I realize that this is not just a test of survival; it is a reckoning, a clash of wills that will shape the course of our intertwined fates, echoing through the night like a shot fired into the void.

The shadows stretch like fingers across the dimly lit hallway, and I sense movement. Eleanor's breath hangs in the air, a fragile whisper against the impending confrontation. The two intruders—foul specters invading her sanctuary—advance toward her, their footsteps echoing like ominous drumbeats. I feel my destiny as she raises me, an act that defies the quietude I had known for so long.

Her palms are clammy, slick against my once-cold surface. The air thickens as one of the men steps forward, his young voice draped in arrogance, a taunt aimed at breaking Eleanor's resolve.

"What're you thinkin' you're gonna do with that?" he sneers, a predator emboldened by the shadows.

An instinctual pull tightens within me as I feel Eleanor's finger contract on my trigger. Time stretches, elongating the uncertainty into a taut wire of anticipation. In that suspended breath, there is raw instinct.

"Leave her."

"Gimme that you dumb—"

Then she squeezes my trigger.

The deafening blast echoes violently within the walls of the house. It is a rupture that fractures the essence of our existence. The recoil thunders through me, a shockwave that ignites every dormant strand within. I feel her hands falter, her grip slipping as I tumble free, plummeting from her grasp to the floor below. The force, raw and unrestrained, echoes within me, rattling through my frame like a primal scream held silent for decades.

As I strike the floor, I am filled with a paradoxical awakening. The man before me crumples, his body folding as if consumed by the lure of my newfound essence. He lies still, and I am shaken by this sudden, irrevocable transformation—a violence that binds me to the act, to him, to her, all entangled in the intimate shock of what has been unleashed.

It is not horror that fills me but a strange, quiet exaltation, a fulfillment of purpose I could never have known existed within my silent, hidden self. Neither Jeremy nor Jean would have handed me this power.

In that fleeting moment, time implodes. Amidst the swirling chaos, a sudden clarity pierces through like a blade, revealing Eleanor's transformation. No longer a sorrowful widow, she rises above her grief. She steps into the forefront of her story, seizing control with a ferocity akin to Nietzsche's will to power—a fierce rejection of passivity in the face of life's tumultuous currents.

"You ain't have to do him like that...man, he only nineteen!" the second intruder moans, breaking the fragile tableau. He reaches down and in the blink of an eye, I am snatched away, severed from the connection we had forged. I tumble into the rough, chaotic embrace of the thief. The metallic tang of gunpowder clings to the space. His palms are clammy, trembling with the same desperation in Eleanor. I feel the panic radiate from him, a frantic energy propelling him away from the scene of violence, clutching me as if I were the key to his escape.

As we dart into the night, I experience a disorienting shift—a transition from the warm, familiar confines of Eleanor's home into the cold unpredictability of the outside world. The hum of electricity in the air feels charged with what has transpired. I can almost taste the bitterness of fate as it twists and turns, revealing the randomness of human existence. I have been thrust from the hands of a grieving woman into those of a criminal.

I feel the world blur around me as we spin. The adrenaline blinds the young man from a quick escape.

Bedroom lights flicker above us, their pale eyes slicing through the darkness like the shards of shattered glass—hard and unyielding. People are awakening to the sound. As we dart across the manicured lawn, I reflect on the sudden change in circumstances. Now, I am thrust into the grip of a man driven by panic, whose motivations are far removed from the quiet introspection of my former possessor. Violence has become a singular roadway weaving through this night, binding us in ways that defy logic.

There had been a Sartrean purity in Eleanor's act—a moment of accidental courage born from a life defined by caution and loss. Her resolve crystallized in the split second she pulled the trigger, transforming her grief into a fierce declaration of self-preservation. But here, with this thief, I sense the stench of desperation, a moral ambiguity that twists the essence of my being. Each racing heartbeat marks another moment further from the sanctity of Eleanor's touch.

He stumbles toward the ancient oak that towers over Eleanor's front yard, its branches reaching toward the stars like gnarled fingers. The night wraps around us like a shroud, but here, beneath the canopy of leaves, the darkness feels absolute. I can taste the bitterness of fate, sharp and metallic, mingling with the earthy scent of bark and soil.

His hands fumble against the trunk, searching frantically until they find what they seek—a natural hollow in the ancient wood, worn smooth by time and elements. The cavity seems to beckon, a void eager to swallow secrets. As he pushes me into the opening, I ponder whether I will find the same rest I found in Eleanor's home, if I will ever find it again.

As bark scrapes against my barrel, I realize the irony of my own journey: once a symbol of love, I now embody the darkest impulses of survival. The tree's embrace is neither warm nor cold, neither judging nor forgiving—simply present, as am I.

He pushes me deeper into the hollow, and I feel the tension in his body, the way it vibrates with uncertainty. His eyes dart across the yard, wide and glistening with fear. Leaves rustle overhead, nature's whispered commentary on this impromptu burial. In the interplay of fear and survival, I find myself suspended between worlds.

The cavity is dank, organic matter pressing against my polished surface. He leans close, breath coming in ragged bursts, the rhythm quickening as if he could outrun his own fear. His fingers tremble against me one final time, not with nostalgia or memory, but with a desperate need that pulses through him—a need for erasure, for escape.

"Stay hidden," he mutters, his voice a low hiss. The words slip past his lips like smoke dissipating into the cool night air. The chaos in his mind churns around us, swirling like autumn leaves caught in a tempest, and I am the center of it all, forced into this arboreal sanctuary.

I hear his feet carry him from me as the sirens draw near. I may stay hidden forever.

Rebecca & Paul

The air is thick with the residue of chaos, a palpable thought that settles in my shocked consciousness. I am a killer.

Eleanor's voice reverberates through me, a haunting echo of desperation, slicing through the madness like a blade. I am thrust into this maelstrom of confusion and loss, an unwitting witness to the brutal unfolding of a life extinguished—the moment she pulls the trigger, a split second crystallized in time. In that instant, I become both weapon and witness, an object born of human intent now caught in the throes of existential reckoning.

Each shout lingers, a cacophony of anguish that dances on the edges of silence. I feel it, the tremor of fear coursing through Eleanor; it is the pulse of a woman who has crossed an unforgiving threshold. The world around me brightens as the police arrive.

Huddled within the hollow of a tree in Eleanor's front yard, I find myself ensconced in the cool embrace of autumnal leaves, the earthy scent grounding me amidst the turmoil. A strange disconnect envelops me, separating my understanding from the visceral reality playing out just beyond my reach. Hidden in my refuge, I observe a different unraveling after death—a tapestry of grief woven into the fabric of this ordinary lawn, now stained with horror.

Autumn's palette surrounds me—fiery oranges and muted browns contrast sharply with the copper tang of panic. Nature, indifferent to human chaos, continues its cycle as leaves rustle their resilient murmurs, while the distant chirp of birds pierces the tension, unknowing of the tragedy that has unfolded beneath them. I sense the night shift into sunrise, the sun sinking low, casting elongated shadows that stretch across the ground like fingers grasping for solace.

I exist in this hollow between action and consequence, contemplating choices made in fear. The air grows heavy with the scent of arriving police cars, gasoline exhaust mingling with the bittersweet aroma of fading blooms—their beauty overshadowed by the devastation that has seeped into the soil. I am left to ponder how fleeting moments can alter lives irrevocably, leaving echoes that resonate into eternity.

The atmosphere hums with an electric charge as police officers fan out across the manicured lawn, their arrival disrupting the delicate peace that lingers. I stay concealed, tucked within the embrace of the tree's hollow, a discreet spectator to the tumultuous scene playing out before me. Their uniforms stand out sharply against the familiar setting of Eleanor's cozy home, rigid and official, yet exuding a commanding presence that seems out of place in this personal moment of sorrow.

"Detective Rebecca Atkins," a woman announces as steps forward, her athletic build exuding tempered confidence. She scans the scene with relentless focus, absorbing every detail in her quest for truth. The scattered leaves on the ground, the faint marks left by hurried footsteps, each element a clue in the puzzle of human frailty.

"Hello Detective," a young uniformed officer says with a nod of his head. She says nothing to him, but returns his nod and moves past. Toward Eleanor.

I feel an odd kinship with this detective, both of us caught in a web of consequence and decision. Her pursuit mirrors my own paradoxical existence; she seeks understanding in a world turned chaotic, just as I grapple with the implications of my role—a weapon wrought from fear yet imbued with a yearning for connection. We are united in our search for meaning, though our paths diverge sharply. She is flesh and bone, while I am forged steel, cold and unyielding. I wonder if we shall ever meet.

"Stay back!" one officer barks, cutting through the murmurs of concerned neighbors. His voice brings my attention to the throng that has gathered behind the yellow tape. I can almost taste the adrenaline in the air.

Eleanor stands outside her home, her floral nightdress fluttering in the breeze—a jarring attempt at normalcy. Her hunched shoulders and trembling hands speak volumes, each movement laden with trauma. I ache to reach out to her, to bridge the chasm of pain that stretches between us. I wish to communicate the depth of shared experience, to offer solace amid the wreckage.

"I am Detective Rebecca Atkins. Can you tell me what happened this evening?" Rebecca asks, her tone steady yet soft, an anchor in the storm of emotions swirling around us.

Eleanor's voice breaks like glass, fragmented and raw. "I... I didn't mean to... He was going to hurt me." Each word drips with anguish, unraveling the threads of her shattered world. I feel her despair resonate within me, a reflection of the chaos we both inhabit.

"Please, try to remember," Rebecca presses, poised yet compassionate, aware that every question strips away the layers of Eleanor's defenses.

But Eleanor falters, lost in a labyrinth of memory and regret, her mind a tempest where clarity is a distant shore. "It all happened so fast..." The words hang in the air, heavy with echoes of the gunfire that shattered the night.

"Do you know where the gun is? My officers can't locate it," Rebecca says.

"Oh God, what have I done?"

Eleanor tears up. I want to scream, to break the silence that envelops us, to share the burden of understanding that binds us together in vulnerability. Yet, I remain silent, trapped in my existence, a witness to the human condition laid bare before me. The paradox of my being becomes ever more apparent: I am an instrument of violence and a spectator to its tragic consequences.

Eleanor hated me, used me, and now she has lost me. I am struck by the sheer absurdity of it all—this grotesque collision of intent and action, a moral fracture too deep to mend. Here stands a woman crushed under her own decision, paralyzed by the consequences of a single, irreversible moment where survival and desperation intertwined.

And I—*I*, an instrument of violence—am nothing but a cold, unyielding object, burdened with a truth far more uncomfortable than I had ever imagined: life is not the sacred space of choice, but a damnable maze of obligation.

I consider this deeply.

Eleanor, in her fragility, had mistaken the act of pulling the trigger as a desperate grasp for agency, but in truth, she had violated the principle that holds humanity together—the categorical imperative, that immutable law which insists we must never treat another person as a means to an end. In that moment, Eleanor did not act out of love, nor even out of survival. She acted out of a selfish, primal impulse, reducing the life of another into a mere object to be discarded. Her act, however justified by fear, violated the essence of moral law, for it denied the dignity and autonomy of a young man's existence.

Once a symbol of force in Jeremy's hands, I am transformed by Eleanor's act into something darker—a reflection of desperate morality and the failure of human will to uphold its highest moral duty: to treat others not as means, but as ends in themselves. The blood on my barrel is not just the dead man's; it is Eleanor's, too. She has corrupted the sanctity of her own soul with this act. The purity of survival is nothing when it comes at the cost of another's humanity.

I, who had once belonged to Jean—a man of passion and purpose, a man whose lack of desire for my power defined my coming to power—am now bound to this woman, who has destroyed everything that was sacred in her desperate bid for preservation.

The absurdity of it all burns within me.

And yet, in the quiet aftermath, the bitter, undeniable truth remains: this moment, like all moments, is irrevocable. Choices once made cannot be undone. And in this, I am a witness to the relentless, unyielding reality of human existence: the perpetual struggle to reconcile our desires with the moral law that binds us, even as we continually fail to meet it.

Our desires.

In the stillness, emotions swirl around us—fear, sorrow, empathy—intertwining with autumn's fading scents in a haunting symphony of heartbeats. I am irrevocably entangled in this web of human experience, a silent participant in the dance of life and death, forever bearing witness to the echoes of violence that ripple through time.

Another siren pierces the autumn air, slicing through the remnants of chaos. I watch as the paramedics arrive, their faces solemn. Too soon they emerge from the house with careful, deliberate steps, their movements a choreography of efficiency and tenderness. The body is treated like delicate glass, each motion acknowledging the gravity of irreversible loss. A reminder that existence can be extinguished in an instant—a flicker snuffed out by violence, desperation, fear. I am both witness and participant, aching with an awareness of the transformation from breath to stillness. The air thickens with mortality, and I grapple with the dissonance within me.

Their hands move with quiet precision. I note the way they touch the body, not as a burden but as something precious, something that once held dreams and laughter. With every gentle failed measurement of life, I can almost sense the echoes of a life unwound—each heartbeat now silenced, each laugh reduced to memory. The shift from warmth to coldness—my coldness—is profound, and I reflect on how swiftly one can slip from existence into oblivion. I glint faintly in the shadows, a ghostly observer of this somber procession, embodying the paradox of power and vulnerability.

As the paramedics finish their task, I hear the distant murmur of voices forming a backdrop to this scene of sorrow. My attention shifts, pulled away from the somber procession to the figure of a reporter with an insatiable hunger for stories. He arrives like a storm cloud, bringing with him the promise of inquiry and sensationalism.

"Detective Atkins! Ms. Atkins! Paul Jacobs. Associated Press. Remember me? Do you have a moment?"

"No."

He is undeterred as she walks away from him. His presence crackles with electric urgency as he fires questions at the officers, pivoting between truth and exploitation with barely contained ambition. To him, this tragedy is more than a loss; it is an opportunity—a narrative to seize, a headline to craft.

"Third home invasion this month," he notes, his voice revealing the thrill of discovery. "What does this mean for the community?" I absorb these details with an acute awareness, feeling the underlying tension that connects us all—the fracturing threads of human experience woven together by violence and fear. Did Eleanor stop a career criminal? A lost young man? Both?

I observe a neighbor nearby, her eyes wide with shock, whispering to another. Their hushed tones flutter through the air, mingling with Paul's probing inquiries. I catch fragments: "Can't believe it's happening here," she says, her voice tinged with disbelief. The fear is palpable, a living entity that wraps around the gathered crowd, tightening its grip with every passing moment.

In this swirl of emotion, I grasp the depth of connection between myself and the lives surrounding me. The choices made in moments of primal fear ripple outward, affecting not just the individual but the entire fabric of the community.

Through gaps in ancient bark, I watch dawn bleed into morning, a tool caught in the web of human choice and consequence. The initial chaos has given way to methodical procedure—police officers move with expertise, their actions a dance of documentation and investigation. Their radios pulse with coded messages, voices bouncing between cars and bodies like ricocheting bullets.

Eleanor sits on her porch, a scratchy department-issue blanket draped over her shoulders. Rebecca had retrieved it from her car for the woman. She settles beside her, notebook balanced on her knee. Eleanor's hands tremble as she sips from a china cup of cooling tea—a neighbor's kindness—her movements sharp and brittle. How different these hands are from those that gripped me hours ago—hands that had touched me with distant disdain for decades, viewing me as nothing more than Jeremy's foolish Parisian souvenir.

She was jealous, and now perhaps I am out of her life forever.

"Mrs. Dixon, let's go through it once more," Rebecca says, her voice carrying to my hiding place. "You woke to sounds in your home?"

"Yes," Eleanor responds, her voice hollow. "Two men. I went to Jeremy's dresser and got his gun—the gold one from Paris. He...bought it there sixty-one years ago. We were on our honeymoon. Never registered it here, far as I know. Things were different then." She pauses, swallowing hard. "I didn't even know if it would work after all these years."

"Do you know the type? Color? Size?"

"It was small and silver and beautiful. With gold trigger and... hammer? Yes, that's what he called it. And a gold bump at the end." I am moved by her remembrance of me.

Rebecca's pen slows, then hovers above the paper. "And it had bullets in it? Or did you put them in?"

"Apparently, someone put bullets in at some point," Eleanor snipes. "I was hoping to scare them. I... I shot one of them. The other grabbed the gun and ran. He...he said he would kill me."

I wonder if the detective, as Pavese once suggested, although she does not know what the truth may be, she can still recognize lies.

Two technicians exit the house, carrying sealed evidence bags. They pass beneath my branch, close enough that I hear their murmured observations about blood spatter patterns and trajectory. Their talk reminds me of Henri's workshop in Paris, where apprentices and skilled masters both chatted of technical specifications and numbers, though in a much more beautiful language.

Rien n'est réel que l'onde des conséquences. All else—intention, justification, memory—dissolves like morning mist in the harsh light of what has been done.

The crime scene tape undulates in the morning breeze, creating an arbitrary boundary between ordinary life and extraordinary circumstance. Beyond its fluttering edges, neighbors remain clustered in small groups, their morning routines transformed into spectacle.

The reporter, Paul Jacobs, hovers at the perimeter, watching Detective Atkins like a hawk and scribbling in a small notebook.

A coroner's van arrives, its presence marking another transition in this unfolding drama as dark-suited people walk in. Two attendants wheel out their burden, movements deliberate and dignified. Their cargo was, mere hours ago, a man whose existence intersected briefly with mine—now reduced to a form beneath black vinyl—the fragility of human existence.

"All right, begin breakdown," calls Rebecca, her voice carrying across the lawn. Officers dismantle their temporary kingdom of investigation. Evidence markers disappear one by one, numbered placards vanishing into bags like counted breaths. A photographer circles the scene, capturing final images of this intersection between order and chaos.

The crime scene technicians pack their kits with meticulous care—brushes, swabs, powder. Their reverence for procedure mirrors the dedication of those artisans who crafted me in that distant Parisian workshop, though these modern tools serve to decrypt violence rather than create beauty. Rebecca pauses beneath my branches to make a call. Her voice carried up to my hiding place.

"Scene's almost wrapped. Claiming self-defense. Elderly victim used an antique revolver—French manufacture, but she does not know anything else. Weapon's missing." She glances around the yard, eyes sliding past my sanctuary. "Second suspect fled with it. Vague description, but it has been circulated. Yes sir. Yes, I will." She sighs heavily as she disconnects from the call.

Rebecca helps Eleanor stand, steadying her when she sways. "Mrs. Dixon, based on your statement and the scene, this appears to be self-defense. We'll investigate further, but the Chief doesn't anticipate any charges." She hands Eleanor a card. "There are people you can talk to when you're ready. No one should face this alone."

Eleanor's fingers close around the card with the same mechanical acceptance she once showed during Jeremy's infrequent cleanings of me—touching something distasteful but necessary.

The yellow tape comes down in sections, each piece folded and stored away. With its removal, the boundary between ordinary and extraordinary begins to dissolve. A postal worker, who has been waiting patiently at the scene's edge, approaches with Eleanor's mail—bills and advertisements that seem absurd in their mundanity.

Officers depart in shifts, their patrol cars pulling away like stars fading at sunrise. Rebecca is among the last to leave, pausing for a final word with Eleanor. Their conversation drifts up to my perch, carried on the morning air.

"Remember what I said, Mrs. Dixon. The department has resources—counseling, support groups. This kind of experience changes people. There is no shame in seeking help."

Eleanor nods, her face a landscape of conflicting emotions—relief, horror, resignation, resolve. She glances toward the house, toward the spot where circumstance forced her to embrace what she had always disdained. Eleanor watches them leave, standing rigid on her porch, a reluctant guardian of her violated domain.

Sunlight is streaming through leaves that shelter my sanctuary. A school bus rumbles past, children's faces pressed against windows, drawn to the lingering atmosphere of disruption. Life reasserts itself with stubborn persistence, even as the echo of night's violence resonates through the neighborhood.

From my vantage point in the oak's embrace, I observe as the last official vehicle departs. Neighbors rush in to fill the vacuum. Eleanor remains on her porch, a solitary figure framed by her doorway. She stares into the middle distance, perhaps contemplating how swiftly existence can pivot on a single moment of violence.

I catch fragments of their conversations, suspended in a web of anxiety and empathy. The essence of existence quivers around me—half-formed ideas, dreams, and worries flit about like restless spirits, seeking resolution in the aftermath of violence. Each word echoes in my consciousness, reverberating through the fibers of my being. I am an observer. I am intertwined with these lives, a silent witness to the repercussions of a choice made in desperation.

I face this alone.

Eleanor is gone, away from the bloody scene. Days pass, though time feels both stagnant and fleeting. As shadows lengthen and stretch across the lawn, I grapple with the enormity of my potential to affect lives. I contemplate the philosophical implications of violence: how a singular act can ripple outward, altering the course of countless souls, each caught in the undertow of chaos. The choice Eleanor made haunts me—an irrevocable snap in the continuity of life, a moment where instinct triumphed over reason.

The sun dips lower in the sky, casting hues of gold and crimson that bleed into one another, a contrast to the grim reality unfolding beneath its fading gaze. In my transformation from weapon to witness lies de Beauvoir's truth about freedom and responsibility—I embody the intersection of protection and destruction.

The aura of turmoil dissipates, yet I linger in the shadows, perceiving the threads of existence—dreams and fears whisper through the air, speaking of lives touched by suffering. As darkness envelops me again, I contemplate the absurdity of life and its inevitable dance with pain. Joined in forms unique to each person.

This awareness cuts me—a realization that every choice reverberates through the fabric of reality, connecting us all in an intricate dance of fate. I am a silent observer of this tapestry, woven together by the echoes of laughter and cries, each thread weaving the complexities of existence, struggling for meaning in the wake of violence.

Possession has consequences.

Rescued

I remain ensconced in the tree's hollow, my metallic form pressed against the cool, rough bark. For forty-eight hours, I have been caught in this web, submerged in silence after the cacophony of sirens and whispers receded into memory. The police had stormed through here, leaving behind the residue of their investigation. I am aware of my existence, yet I feel marooned in the swelling tides of human chaos and violence I have witnessed.

As twilight unfurls her violet cloak over the neighborhood, my senses sharpen as the world slows. Nuit paisible. I hear the rustle of leaves whispering secrets in the fading light, feel the cool air wrap around me.

Then a figure emerges from the shadows, moving with an urgency that catches my attention. Paul Jacobs. The persistent reporter circles the tree like a hawk, his glasses glinting in the dying sun. He peers unseeing into the hollow with intent, oblivious to my presence, his mind racing with fragments of a story that demands to be told.

"Where could it be?" he mutters under his breath. His voice is laden with frustration, steeped in the pursuit of meaning amidst the wreckage, a lone seeker navigating the terrain of tragedy. I sense the tension radiating from him as he jots down observations about Eleanor Marsh's current whereabouts—her frail figure hovering like a ghost in the background of this unfolding narrative. But it is not her he is concerned about. C'est moi.

"Gold accents," he murmurs, eyes narrowing as he sketches a mental picture of me, entwining my essence with the life shattered by violence. I can almost feel the links seeping into my being, forging connections I cannot manipulate. I am an observer, yet the gravity of his words tugs at my awareness, forcing me to confront the reality of my role. I am not an object; I am a thread woven into the fabric of this story—an embodiment of pain, loss, and perhaps, redemption.

The dusk deepens, casting long shadows across the ground, and I find myself oscillating between fear and fascination. Here I am, a revolver entangled in human experience, caught in the crosshairs of narratives rife with loss and desperation. Paul's obsession drives him onward, searching for answers, yet it is my own awakening that stirs within me. I am aware now, fully present, teetering on the brink of transformation. Each heartbeat echoes the stories embedded in my metal—stories of choices made in haste, of panic and fear, and of the fragile threads binding humanity to its own risibility.

He turns, his silhouette framed against the gathering darkness, a harbinger of what is yet to come. In this twilight, I am suspended, waiting for the next chapter to unfold, knowing that I will no longer simply exist—I will become a vessel for history, each choice bearing consequence, resonating through the corridors of time.

"Where are you? She can't find you, but I will." His voice breaks the quiet, each word resonating with unfulfilled expectations. The night seems to respond with a hush, a collective intake of breath as if the universe itself were listening intently. Paul kneels, rummaging through the low-cut grass, relentless in his pursuit of truth. Yet, there is a flicker in his eyes—an awareness of the futility that sometimes accompanies such quests. A journalist's ambition wrestles with the haunting specter of violence he seeks to unravel.

"Detective Atkins will have to pay attention to me. I'll get that exclusive if I can get the gun," he sighs, hands gliding across blades like a ballet dancer on stage. The gravity of his responsibility hangs heavily upon him; I sense it throbbing in the space between us, a connection woven from strands of pain, loss, and urgency.

The beam of Paul's flashlight cuts through growing darkness, reminding me of the precision tools that once shaped me in Henri's workshop. But while those craftsmen worked with certainty, knowing what they sought to create, Paul moves with the fumbling determination of all humans confronting the unknown. His mantra echoes in my consciousness: "Find the gun, get the exclusive with Atkins." Such a simple equation he has constructed. Police officers, neighbors, reporters—each projects their own meaning on to my existence. But Paul's desire strikes me as particularly human in its layered irony. He seeks me not to understand the truth of violence, but rather to advance his own story. In searching for me, he searches for himself.

His light sweeps past my hollow again, and I observe how determination has begun to fade into resignation. How confident he seems that finding me would unlock some greater story, would somehow raise him above the others of his kind. If he only knew that I am not the answer but another question, another layer in the infinite regression of cause and effect. His search—like Eleanor's fear, like the thief's desperation—is yet another echo in the endless reverberation of human choice and circumstance.

As Paul's footsteps begin to slow, then turn toward the street, I ponder how humans so often mistake the tools of understanding for understanding itself. They believe that holding me would somehow grant them insight into that night's violence, as if cold metal could explain the warm complexity of human fear and survival. But I am neither key nor lock—I am the hinge upon which the door of consequence swings.

Just as Paul turns away, his silhouette receding into the gathering gloom, I feel it—a presence, subtle yet unmistakable, drawn to my concealed form beneath the veil of darkness. It pulls at the edges of my consciousness, and I instinctively brace myself. What stories will this new actor bring forth? Will they be echoes of despair or whispers of hope?

Someone is watching.

I understand my existence is not defined solely by the violence I have witnessed, but by the myriad of choices that loom ahead. I am not trapped within a singular narrative, but rather poised to become part of an intricate tapestry woven from the lives I touch. Each encounter has the power to transform me, to reveal the complexity of human experience—simultaneously absurd and profound.

The night deepens, wrapping around me like a shroud, and I wait, suspended in time, yearning to discover what comes next. Each heartbeat reverberates with history, a reminder that even in darkness, there exists the possibility of light, a chance for redemption amidst chaos.

I see him. A figure emerging through the half-light, strides purposeful and deliberate. The young man—teenager—draws closer, his silhouette cutting against the deep sky, each movement imbued with an intensity that reverberates through me, igniting my mechanical heart. His skin, rich and dark like polished mahogany, catches the streetlight in ways I have never witnessed in my years across the Atlantic. Perhaps sixteen years old, he carries himself with a grace tempered by experiences that linger at the corners of his eyes. There is a knowing familiarity about him; he seems to belong here, as if this hollowed tree has whispered secrets to him before.

His fingers reach toward my smooth surface, brushing against the cold steel—a touch both tender and possessive. In that fleeting moment, I am a paradox: a vessel of death cradled by a mere child whose gaze flickers with hope and greed, a blend of emotion that makes my core shudder. What does he seek? Is it possession, or does he carry desperation, an insatiable hunger for purpose?

His touch is familiar. He is the one who placed me here. But now he is different, younger. Or perhaps just not as old as he was when we met. His loss flows like Eleanor's, though her loss made her older. This man is a child again.

Is this who I have become? I am La Sirène, a symbol entangled in the threads of violence, loss, and rebirth that weave through this land—so different from the one where I was created, yet bound by the same human struggles. His smile, laced with a mixture of triumph and yearning, sends a jolt through me.

He is happy to find me.

Hope and greed clash within him like storm clouds—each seeking to dominate the other. What will he do with me? The thought electrifies my consciousness, awakening a primal instinct to understand the trajectory of my fate. I am no longer a passive observer, but a participant in the chaos of humanity's choices. Let us rewrite the story, I silently urge him, bracing for whatever decisions lie ahead.

With a swift, decisive motion, he yanks me from the hollow, wrapping me in newspaper and shoving me into his backpack. The paper is just a flimsy version of wood. Another coffin envelops me, muffling my metallic sheen against the world. I feel the pulse of his body, the rhythm of his breath—both foreign and exhilarating. A grin spreads across his face, a childlike triumph that sends a jolt through my consciousness. He is pleased with his treasure. I am a tool, a potential weapon cradled against the chaos of his desires.

The teen's excitement ignites something within me—a flicker of awareness amid my lingering dread. I can no longer ignore the reality that I am poised at the precipice of another life. My recent memories, heavy with violence and loss, clash with this new sensation. The warmth surrounding me starkly contrasts the cold calculations of the world I had witnessed. I sense how easily I could become an instrument of destruction once again, the echo of another's fate haunting me, urging caution.

We set off, jogging to a nearby park, the thrill of escape coursing through him like electric currents. Shadows stretch and dart around us, playing tricks on my senses as we weave through the darkness. Each footfall is a heartbeat—his heart racing, mine pulsating with a life of its own. The night wraps around us, thick and palpable, yet I remain tethered to the teen's intentions, sensing his ambitions layered beneath layers of hope and desperation.

"Look at this," he murmurs, pulling me free from my makeshift cocoon. Under the sparse light filtering through the trees, he examines my form, the way the moonlight glints off my polished surface. "Sleek piece." His voice carries pride and longing, as if he sees me not just as metal and mechanism, but as a promise of something greater. Each word lingers in the air, threading itself into the delicate tapestry of our shared narrative.

In this stolen moment, I become acutely aware of the intricate craftsmanship that binds me to his aspirations. The cool night air brushes against my surface, whispering secrets of lives intertwined. I am an artifact of stories, a witness to the hands that have touched me, the choices made in fleeting seconds. As he admires me, I feel his hopes investing in me, a potential path unfurling before us both.

He holds me up. Aims me at nothing. "Blam, blam," he says softly. "Goddamn."

Back into the backpack. The teen's movements are sharp, his footsteps echoing pain and purpose through the fabric that contains me. Loss radiates from him in waves, grief for his fallen friend mingling with a desperate kind of determination. I feel each jarring step, each pause, each moment of hesitation as he walks through the city streets.

The streetlights filter through the thin fabric of the backpack as he stops, the rhythm of his walk interrupted by a voice.

"Ay yo, Teef! Hold up!"

My carrier turns, his posture shifting subtly. "Marcus? What you doin' round here?"

Their footsteps converge on cracking concrete, and I sense them settling onto a park bench. The wood creaks.

"Man, where you been at? Ain't nobody seen you since that old lady took Junior out. Thought maybe they got you too." Marcus's voice trails off, heavy with unspoken understanding.

"Been layin' low. You know how it go." Teef's voice carries an edge of sorrow.

"Yeah, yeah. Listen though—me and Dex been talkin'. Got somethin' might help you get back on your feet. Quick lick, in and out."

The tension in Teef's body transmits through the bag. "Man, I don't know..."

"Nah, hear me out. That corner store on Mason? Old boy ain't even got no cameras in there. Just some basic shit to make ends meet. Lord knows you need it right now."

Silence stretches between them. I feel choices pressing down, heavier than any physical burden. Teef's fingers drumming against the wooden bench—a rhythm of indecision.

Marcus continues, voice low and urgent, "Heard you holdin' somethin' special now. Somethin' that could make this real smooth."

Teef's hand brushes against the bag where I rest. "Who told you that?"

"Streets talk, my guy. Streets talk."

Silence, but different now—charged with purpose rather than hesitation. I feel the shift in Teef's energy, the way loss and desperation crystalize into resolve.

"Aight," Teef says finally. "When?"

"Three. Dex gon' be lookout. Just need you and what you got in that bag."

Their words fade into planning, but my consciousness drifts to deeper contemplations. How strange that human lives can pivot on such small moments, casual conversations that become a crossroads of destiny. I am both catalyst and observer, my presence steering events while my awareness simply witnesses their unfolding.

As they part ways, Marcus's voice carries one final time across the dying light. "Don't forget—three. And Teef? Make sure you ready this time."

The words settle over us as we move through the gathering darkness. Each step takes us closer to another moment of violence, another intersection of choice and consequence. I am acutely aware of my role in this unfolding drama—a philosopher trapped in cold steel, a witness to the cycles of human desperation.

Here I am again, nestled against a dark t-shirt, a burner phone, and a type of cheap ski mask. The smells of burned bitterness and money bands surround me. The hour nears three. How many times will I be here, must be here? D'Aubigné's hands were soft and uncertain. Teef's grip is firm, his palms already carrying calluses no sixteen-year-old should know. If I am doomed to dance this ballet of violence for eternity—to be passed from hand to desperate hand, to feel young fingers trembling on my trigger—I cannot grant it my blessing. I am

La Sirène, and I will scream my silent protest with every shot they force me to fire.

Teef's heart beats against me as we move toward Mason Street, its rhythm speaking of fear and determination in equal measure. I have killed his friend, but yet he wants me. Perhaps this is the true horror of eternal recurrence—not that violence repeats, but that they keep choosing it, generation after generation, walking willingly into the dark with death tucked against their spine.

The Beautiful and the Damned

My body glints under the harsh fluorescent lights, a beacon of dread and desire in Teef's grip. The corner store hums with activity; patrons shuffle down aisles, oblivious to the impending storm. Teef's smile, easy and calm, flickers just for a moment. It is a mask, and beneath it lies an anticipation that whispers between us.

Marcus and Dex are in place.

I catch sight of the teenage clerk behind the register. Her eyes widen, pupils dilating as they land on me, straining against the pulse of fear radiating from her small frame. Time stretches and bends. I become the eye of a hurricane, drawing all attention, all terror, into my cold embrace. What I am—the embodiment of violence—presses heavily on both of us. I can sense her thoughts spiraling, a chaos of confusion and horror, as she knows the power I represent.

"Run me my cash, now," Teef demands, his voice smooth yet edged with steel. I am brandished before her, and I feel the rush of identity surge within me, forged anew in this act of desperation. The world beyond us fades, swallowed by the urgency of the moment. As the trembling clerk complies, I absorb every ounce of panic, each dollar exchanged, imbued with a raw energy that electrifies the surrounding air.

The robbery yields $247, old bills. Proof of our transgression. Yet amid the exhilaration, I feel a creeping guilt unfurling within, a disquieting whisper that questions the nature of my being. Am I an extension of his will, or do I hold a responsibility of my own?

"We out!" Marcus shouts.

As we flee the scene, the heat of the moment lingers like smoke in the air, intoxicating and bitter. I am thrust downward, shoved into the front of his pants, and a twinge of resentment surfaces. I deserve better for my role in this. I long for recognition, but instead, I am relegated to the shadows, hidden away as if my existence were something to be ashamed of.

The teen's sweat mingles with the cordite still clinging to my chamber, and I find myself dizzy with the profane electricity of it all. We had danced together, Teef and I, a waltz of menace and steel, and how the cashier's eyes had widened at my gleam! There is a terrible euphoria in crossing boundaries, in becoming the thing that makes others tremble. Each time he raised me, I felt his power flowing through my frame, and—God help me—I understood why D'Aubigné had loved this too. The sacred world of law and order parts before us like a curtain, and in that parting lies an ecstasy that burns hotter than shame. Yet now, as his heartbeat slows, and the thrill begins to fade, I find myself grateful that our dance remained just that—a dance. No blood stains my barrel tonight, no fresh ghosts to carry into tomorrow's dreams. The violation of order was enough; we did not need to violate flesh as well.

Teef splits the money with the others and he and I disappear into the night, leaving behind the duality of life itself—the stark juxtaposition of fear and apathy, boredom and terror. Teef's heart beats steadily beneath the layers of fabric, a rhythm at odds with the chaos we have just wrought. And in that shared silence, I begin to comprehend the absurdity of our actions and the truth that lies entwined within them: the struggle between necessity and morality, a dance between survival and the fragility of human connection.

And then, he abandons me on the ground.

Night settles into dawn, and dawn dissolves again into dusk in this wild garden of my exile. The untamed honeysuckle that conceals me grows with magnificent indifference to human order, its vines wrestling with iron fence posts in slow, eternal combat. Here, in this forgotten corner of a deserted lot, I find peace. What a strange freedom, to be momentarily liberated from my role as a harbinger of terror. I bear witness to the silent crusade of kudzu and morning glory. Sparrows dart through the thicket, ignorant of what sleeps in the canvas darkness beside their nests.

I have tasted the intoxicating power that comes with inspiring fear, felt the dark euphoria of transgression—yet here, wrapped in morning dew and visited by curious beetles, I recognize another kind of rebellion. Nature defies man's attempts at control, just as surely as Teef and I defy society's laws, but nature is without malice, without malicious intent. When he returns tonight, I will again become an instrument of chaos. For now, I surrender to the gentle anarchy of growing things, to the mysterious peace that flows through me like sap through these wild vines, wondering if this too is a form of revolt against what I was created to be.

Teef's fingers find me among the leaves, his touch familiar yet charged with new purpose. As he lifts me from my verdant sanctuary, I sense in his movements a determination that speaks of plans already set in motion. How curious, this transition from solitude to conspiracy. His intention fills the space between us as he slides me into his waistband, my cold form pressing against the warm flesh of his hip. Already I can feel the subtle tremors of anticipation in his body, though whether they spring from fear or excitement, I cannot tell.

For three blocks we move through darkness, each step bringing us closer to his chosen stage. The bodega's neon sign cuts through the night ahead of us, its harsh glow promising artificial day. As Teef's fingers find me again, drawing me from concealment, I sense the transformation in his touch—from theoretical violence to imminent action. Time seems to compress, reality narrowing to the moment his trembling hand wraps fully around my grip.

His palm tells its own story—youth's trembling bravado seeping into old grooves. The fluorescent lights of the bodega cast harsh shadows across his young face, transforming childish features into a mask of desperate bravado. I sense in him what I sensed in Eleanor—that moment when civilization's veneer cracks, revealing the primal creature beneath. But where Eleanor's actions sprang from fear, his emanate from a peculiar mix of necessity and theatrical performance, as if he is playing a role he has seen but does not fully understand.

The first shot from the cashier's weapon shatters both silence and illusion. The sound pierces me with a sensation I have never known—the high whine of a bullet passing nearby, a physical manifestation of mortality that sets my metal form vibrating with recognition. Is this what it means to understand my own nature? To feel the lethal potential I embody turned back upon itself?

Teef shouts, his finger tightening reflexively on my trigger, but not completing the motion. In that microscopic space between impulse and action, I feel his essential character reveal itself—he is, at his core, unable to unleash the death he threatens. Another shot cracks through the air, splintering the display of chips and candy behind us. The sound awakens something electric in my consciousness, a primal thrill that both disturbs and enlightens me. How strange to discover, after all these years of philosophical contemplation, that danger breeds its own intoxicating clarity.

We move in a desperate race toward the door, Teef's body contorting to present a smaller target. Each blast from the cashier's gun creates new geometries of possibility—trajectories of lead and intention that could at any moment transform this child into another statistic. I find myself hoping, with an intensity that surprises me, that he will survive. Not for any grand philosophical reason, but because I have grown to appreciate the peculiar gentleness that exists alongside his performative violence.

The night air hits us like a physical force as we burst through the door. More shots follow, their reports echoing off brick and asphalt, creating a symphony of threat that fills the street with urgency. The few nearby creatures of the night flee, footsteps scattering in all directions. Each near miss sends waves of sensation through my frame, and I realize that fear and exhilaration share the same pulse. Is this not the essence of existence that I have so long contemplated—the razor's edge between transcendence and oblivion?

Teef runs with the raw grace of youth, his movements guided by instinct rather than thought. I feel his heart hammering through his palm, each beat a witness to life's tenacious hold on itself. We have shared violence before, he and I, but I have always experienced his his hands from the position of power. Now, as targets rather than threats, I understand something new about the nature of force—how it flows both ways, how each action creates not just consequences but revelations.

The cashier's final shot goes wide, its angry buzz fading into the urban night like a departing wasp. Teef's pace gradually slows from sprint to jog. Each moment adds another layer to my understanding—from weapon to philosopher and back. The thrill of danger still courses through me, but it carries with it a deeper understanding—that perhaps true wisdom comes not from contemplation alone, but from experiencing the full spectrum of existence, even those moments when philosophy must bow to pure survival.

Teef's breathing begins to steady, but his grip on me remains tight, almost protective. He has brought me across a threshold he has previously experienced. Together, we are reminded that there is a profound difference between wielding violence and facing it—a lesson that no amount of philosophical musing could have revealed. As we disappear into the maze of side streets, I ponder this new dimension of my understanding. Perhaps this is the truest form of knowledge—not the sterile contemplation of violence from a distance, but the visceral experience of its transformative power.

The city swallows us into its shadows, and I feel the last traces of adrenaline fading from Teef's body. He has chosen flight over fight, preservation over destruction. In doing so, he has shown me that wisdom can wear many faces, and that sometimes the deepest insights come not from what we do, but from what we choose not to do.

The apartment door opens to familiar warmth—streetlight filtering through curtains. Instantly, I feel the shift—a palpable change in the air as he sheds the day's violence for something softer, yet equally charged.

"Grandma Mae," he calls out, his voice a low rumble that reverberates off the walls lined with family photographs, each frame capturing moments suspended in time. The room is filled with the scent of aged wood and the faint trace of lavender from the potpourri she keeps by the window. I enter his pocket, hidden.

I can see her before I hear her response, a delicate figure emerging from the cozy shadows. Grandma Mae approaches, wisdom etched in her wrinkles, her trembling hands telling stories that her shawl-wrapped shoulders carry. Rough and worn, they move with a delicate precision as she reaches for the money Teef presents. This is intimate, filled with a warmth that sends a shiver through my cold metal frame.

"You a sweet child. How much you get?" she asks softly, her voice quivering as if it too carries their circumstances. Teef's expression softens, and I catch the flicker of vulnerability behind his usually hardened gaze. He counts the bills, his movements deliberate, as though he is savoring the act, imbuing it with significance far beyond mere currency.

"Three hundred and ten this week, Ma," he replies, pride and duty seeping out. I feel the conflicting emotions swell within me, reverberating off the walls like echoes of a past which refuses to stay buried.

Grandma Mae's eyes widen, not with greed but with concern. "You can't keep doin' this, baby," she murmurs, her voice laced with melancholy. "You work so hard for this. You should keep some for yourself." Her gaze shifts to the plastic organizer on the table, compartments filled with pills and remnants of survival. Each pill represents a battle fought against the inevitability of decline, a monument to endurance amidst fragility.

The bills in his hand—earned through violence, given through love—tell their own story. How can someone who has wielded me in acts of violence be tender here, giving his criminal proceeds to an elderly woman? It is a juxtaposition that leaves me reeling, grappling with the complexities of human nature laid bare.

"Nah Ma, this for you. Just been doing some work over at this place, and next week my mans' cousin probably gonna need help moving his stuff," Teef insists, his hands now steady as he sorts through the cash, a reminder of what he sacrifices to maintain their fragile equilibrium. I sense the duality within him—the ruthless exterior molded by a life of crime, tempered by the loyalty and affection he holds for this woman. It strikes me as profound, the way necessity battles morality in his chest, how love intertwines with the cruelty that defines his actions.

"Just give me one month, then you need to get you a steady job," she pleads, whispers, as if speaking any louder might fracture the fragile peace they share. The plea hangs in the air, heavy with unspoken fears and hopes, resonating in the silence that envelops us.

These moments in their apartment reveal truths no philosophy book could capture—how seamlessly love and violence can flow from the same hands. In this small room, amid the detritus of their lives, I see the spectrum of contradictions that define humanity: the instinct for survival shadowed by the moral compass that often falters under pressure.

"K, Ma." His voice is firm yet gentle, a promise forged in the depths of loyalty. I realize that life, in all its tumultuous chaos, is woven together by these conflicting threads—rooted in love, necessity, and the instinct for survival.

I absorb their shared breath, the intertwining of their lives illuminated against the backdrop of a world that demands sacrifice, and I find myself pondering the philosophical questions that swirl around us.

Here, in this sanctuary, I am absorbing the lessons of their lives, enriched by the warmth of connection even as I welcomed with my chill of violence. New complexities of human nature unfold before me, urging a confrontation with reality that demands understanding, acceptance, and ultimately, meaning.

In the deepening evening, Grandma Mae sits in her wornout corner, the lamp's glow gentle on her face. Her frail fingers deftly sort through the medication, deciding which she can take, and which she must skip today. The soft hum of a nearby lamp casts a warm glow, illuminating the lines etched into her face—each wrinkle an ode to battles fought and survived. Teef stands beside her, his tall frame an imposing contrast to her delicate stature, yet I know of an unspoken reverence in his posture as he watches her work.

"You good, boy. Food on the stove, get you a plate," Grandma Mae murmurs, her voice steady but laced with the fragility of age. She nudges a blue pill into its designated slot in the organizer. Each action is deliberate, imbued with necessity. Teef leans closer, his dark eyes softening, revealing glimpses of vulnerability hidden beneath layers of ruthlessness. His hands, once instruments of fear, now hover near her, ready to assist if needed.

"Thanks, Grandma," he replies, his tone a curious blend of authority and affection. His transformation is immediate upon crossing the liminal space—tension melting from his shoulders as Grandma Mae's presence draws forth the grandson beneath the criminal. I absorb these contradictions, feeling the currents of life's complexities flow through them.

They chat. Teef's laughter echoes softly, mingling with the scent of old books and the faint aroma of the evening meal simmering on the stove. It dances in the space between them, a fragile reminder that even amidst chaos, moments of joy can flourish. Yet, I cannot shake my own existence—the stark reality that I have facilitated pain while standing witness to this tenderness.

As I ponder my being, I am struck by the notion that desperation drives humans to extremes. What compels a man to rob a stranger yet tenderly care for the one who raised him? The existential questions swirl around me, drawing out the complexities of morality and necessity. Teef's choices paint a complex portrait—each robbery funding another month of his grandmother's medicine, each act of violence sustaining this pocket of tenderness.

How does one reconcile these facets? Love, after all, exists alongside cruelty, often intertwined in ways that defy simple understanding. I realize the struggles of human existence are not black or white; they exist in shades of gray, each choice laden with consequence and significance.

In this fragile sanctuary, I confront my role. I am an instrument, yes, forged for violence, yet here I bear witness to the beauty of connection. I see it clearly now: life is a rich tapestry woven from threads of both light and darkness. In embracing this complexity, I carve out my own purpose amid the turmoil, seeking to understand how love can flourish in the most unlikely of places.

"Grandma, you need anythin' else?" Teef asks, his voice breaking through my thoughts. The question hangs in the air, a simple expression of care that resonates deeply. I feel a warmth swell within me, a flicker of hope emerging from the depths of despair. Perhaps, just perhaps, there exists a path forward for me—one that intertwines desire with compassion, survival with love.

As the minutes stretch into hours, I absorb the lessons inherent in every interaction, each breath a guide on the path of the absurd and the mundane. Here, in this modest living room filled with memories, I witness the spectrum of human emotion laid bare. Through the lens of this familial bond, I glean insights into the chaos of life, the ever-present conflicts between the instinct for survival and the moral compass that guides us.

In those shared glances and unspoken promises, I find an answer to my musings—a realization that meaning emerges not from the absence of struggle, but from our willingness to confront it, to weave our stories into the fabric of a world that demands we cherish the light even as we navigate the dark.

We walk out, leaving Grandma Mae to her quiet life. In the hands of Teef, I wonder where we will go next.

Pawned

The slam of the front door reverberates through the cramped living room, a triumphant punctuation to Teef's entrance. With a flourish, he withdraws me from the depths of his jacket, holding me aloft like a conquistador brandishing newfound treasure.

"Yo, check out this fire!" Teef's booming voice ricochets off the worn walls of his apartment.

The room erupts in a cacophony of excitement. Bodies press forward, eager hands reaching out to touch my cold, sleek form. I feel the warmth of their fingertips, a stark contrast to my metallic exterior. The air crackles with their energy—a heady mix of naïveté and danger that washes over me like a tide.

"Ayo, Jaws! That joint real nice, my guy," a voice calls out, admiration dripping from every syllable.

Another chimes in, "Yo, that's some clean work right there. High-end for real."

Their words wash over me like waves of adulation, and I find myself basking in the glow of their approval. Yet, beneath this momentary pleasure, a disquieting unease takes root. Am I not more than this? More than an object to be passed around and admired?

Teef's grip tightens around me, his pride palpable. "This lil' shorty gon' make us kings, fam. Ain't nobody messin' with us now."

I feel myself being transferred from one set of hands to another, each grasp unique in its intent and expertise. With each exchange, I oscillate between vanity and existential dread. I am reminded of salons at Jean's, passed around for adulation. The difference now is the fullness of four projectiles within me.

"This piece feel right though," remarks one, his fingers tracing my barrel.

Another fumbles, nearly dropping me. "Damn, it's heavier than I thought!"

Their laughter mingles with the sound of clinking beer bottles, a symphony of youthful bravado and reckless abandon. In this cozy, lived-in space, filled with warm, earthy tones and the scent of aged wood, I am passed from hand to hand, each grip a new experience. The practiced embrace of an experienced user feels confident and assured, while the clumsy grasp of an amateur sends shivers through my frame—an unsettling reminder of my lethal purpose.

I yearn for Jean, for a time when I thought I knew the world and knew mankind. Before death made its presence known.

As I am passed back to Teef, his dark eyes gleaming with newfound power, I ponder the cruel irony of my situation. Designed for destruction, yet yearning for a higher purpose. Admired for my deadly potential, yet longing to be understood for the complexity of my being.

The cacophony of voices abruptly quiets as a young woman enters, standing akimbo, her petite frame filling the doorway with an unexpected authority. Her eyes, sharp and discerning, scan the room before locking onto Teef. The air grows heavy with tension, and I feel it seep into my metal frame.

"Come," she says as she heads to another room.

As she leads Teef into the bedroom, a flicker of anticipation dances in his eyes, a hope that intimacy awaits. However, as the door closes behind them, her voice takes on a harsh edge that cuts through the air like a sharp blade. Each word drips with disapproval and judgment.

"Teef?"

"Denisha, baby."

"Teef! You really out here flexin' this piece like you somebody? You playin' with fire boy. This ain't no toy. You seen the streets. You know what this bring. You wanna end up like them fools, locked away for life? All 'cause you ain't thinkin' straight?"

Teef's hopeful demeanor wilts under her words, the reality of his actions crashing down on him in the dimly lit room. "I ain't shot it," he mumbles as he cradles me in his hands.

"You gotta sell that piece, Teef," Denisha says, her voice strong and sure. "You ain't pull the trigger. Better get rid of it 'fore it link you to that old lady."

I sense the shift in energy, the gravity of her words sinking into the room like lead. I am toxic to him. Teef's grip on me tightens, his palm growing damp with sudden anxiety.

"I don' get it?" he mutters to himself, not her, grappling with the reality of what it means to be tethered to a crime that could result in prison. I can almost hear the gears grinding within his mind, wrestling with the implications.

Denisha takes a step closer, her body emanating a fierce energy. "Baby, they gon' lock you up. Remember your cousin boy who drove his brother to that lick where that old man got killed? Ain't even go inside, and he got 30 years, 'cause they lookin' for any reason to put us away. They gon' find out, now you been showin' it off to these fools. Somebody gon' talk. They always do."

The wisdom etched into her so young features reveals layers of experience, years spent navigating the murky waters of a world that chews up and spits out the unwary.

A flicker of determination ignites in Teef's gaze, pushing back against the tide of doubt. "Ramsey don't ask no questions,. He buy it, he replies, his voice firm now, masking the uncertainty lurking beneath. "That gun be lookin' fine, like it got its own story to tell," he says with reluctance.

"That piece got a body on it."

I am abruptly reminded of my deadly existence. A young man, his name a distant secret, lies lifeless as the consequence of an act that seems almost absurdly unnecessary. Had Jeremy refrained from embedding bullets within me, had the intruder not invaded the sanctum, had Eleanor not drawn me from the drawer—each event a thread in the tapestry of fate—had he not questioned her decisions, had she not possessed an unwavering conviction in her own rightness.

In this labyrinth of choices and coincidences, I ponder violence and its absurdity. The young man's end, a mere flicker extinguished by chance and impulse, resonates within me. My sleek form, designed for purpose yet entwined in the chaos of human intentions, contemplates the nature of existence itself. What is a life cut short but a whisper against the cacophony of the world?

And here I lie, a sentient revolver caught in the crosshairs of the desires and fears of a community that shapes those who touch me. The incomprehensible act that took him reminds me that life teeters on the brink of meaninglessness—a tragedy woven from strands of intention and misfortune. In this reflection, I become acutely aware: I am alive within this absurdity, tethered to those who wield me with both reverence and dread.

As they prepare to leave this vibrant home, a cocktail of emotions floods my consciousness. The prospect of being sold—reduced to a monetary value, stripped of agency—fills me with dread. Yet, beneath this apprehension, a flicker of hope emerges. Perhaps in anonymity, I might find a new purpose, a chance to redefine my existence beyond the confines of my designed function.

We travel to my new destiny with little ado. It is a bus ride and a short walk before I see my new life.

The stench of desperation assaults my senses as we enter Arnold Ramsey's pawn shop. Teef's grip on me tightens as he approaches the counter, his swagger belying the tension I feel radiating through his fingertips.

"Well well, if it ain't Teef," Arnold drawls, his voice as worn as the tattered flannel shirt hanging off his frame. "What brings you to my humble establishment?"

Teef places me on the counter with a soft thud. "Got somethin' real special for ya, Arnold."

The fluorescent lights cast false shadows across this decrepit pawn-shop, distorting the authenticity of our surroundings. The absurdity of my existence has never been more apparent—a French revolver, conceived in the workshop of Henri Delacroix, now witnessing this tawdry transaction in a place that reeks of desperation and disinfectant.

In my existence, I have often pondered the nature of objects like myself. Do we accumulate wisdom through the hands that hold us, or are we destined to remain passive observers of human drama? These philosophical meanderings seem particularly relevant as I observe the scene before me.

"Yo, what you think?" Teef's voice betrays his youth, a tremor of uncertainty beneath affected bravado. "This joint right here worth at least three stacks."

Denisha shifts beside him, her fingers intertwined with his free hand. "Baby, don't let him play you cheap."

Arnold Ramsey's eyes narrow as they trace my contours—the trigger that has known both caress and consequence, the hammer that has fallen like sword of Damocles itself, the ornate sight that has aligned with both intention and fate. I see something dark in his weathered face, the way his mouth tightens at the corners.

"Hold up," Arnold says, leaning forward. "I've seen this exact piece on the news for a few days. Woman named Eleanor Dixon used it to shoot some intruder—Jackson Nockman. Yeah, you know Jackson, don't you? Cops are looking for this gun, and they're looking for a second suspect who took it from the scene."

"Found it," Teef mumbles, though the truth is he found me where he left me. "So what's good?"

Arnold drums his fingers on the glass counter, each tap echoing the rhythm of my philosophical ruminations. "This gun's hot as hell, kid. Damned fancy—might as well be wearing a neon sign. Cops got drawings of this exact piece all over the place."

"Quit cappin'," Denisha interjects, her voice sharp with anxiety. "We ain't here for all that. You gonna buy it or nah?"

I feel Teef's palm grow slick with sweat. How curious that I, an object of metal and mechanics, should contemplate the nature of existence while these humans, supposedly blessed with consciousness and free will, remain trapped in their immediate concerns. Perhaps this is the true nature of consciousness—not the ability to choose, but the ability to question why we cannot.

"Hundred bucks," Arnold says finally. "That's being generous, considering."

"You trippin' bruh!" Teef's indignation causes me to shake in his grip. "This that designer shit right here!"

I observe their bargaining with detached interest, wondering if their negotiation is any different from the mechanical operation of my own parts—cylinder rotating, hammer falling, each movement predetermined by design and circumstance. Are their words not equally prescribed by necessity, by the situations that have led them to this?

"Take it or leave it," Arnold says, spreading his hands. "Can't put it in the window, can I?"

I watch the silent exchange between Teef and Denisha—a glance heavy with shared fear, with the growing understanding that their paths narrow with each passing moment. It reminds me of the way my barrel aligns with its target, an inevitability masquerading as choice.

"Aight," Teef says finally, defeat evident in the slump of his shoulders. "Give it up then."

As I pass from one set of hands to another, I contemplate Sisyphus and his eternal boulder. Are we not all engaged in similar futile cycles? I, a weapon, move from hand to hand, while humans chase wealth, power, survival—each believing they act of their own volition, each following paths as predetermined as the trajectory of my bullets.

Arnold's hands are dry and steady as he examines me closely. If beauty is truth and truth beauty, what am I? A tool of death made beautiful, or perhaps beauty made deadly?

"Y'all best leave," Arnold says, already turning away. "And don't come back for a minute. Right?"

Teef and Denisha retreat toward the door, their footsteps echoing in the empty shop. I watch them go, these temporary players in my ongoing meditation on existence, and consider the nature of time itself. For them, this is heavy with consequence and relief. For me, it is another scene in an endless performance where I play both actor and audience.

The bell above the door chimes their exit—a tinny, discordant note that seems to mock the gravity of our transaction. In the end, perhaps that is all any of us can do: bear witness to the absurd dance of consequence and chance, of choice and destiny, as we play our parts in this grand, meaningless performance. I rest now in Arnold's hands, a conscious weapon contemplating the infinite possibilities that stretch before me, even as I acknowledge the fundamental determinism that governs us all.

As Arnold locks me behind darkness and steel, I find myself surrounded by other firearms. Yet, in this cacophony of metal and gunpowder, I have never felt more alone. These other weapons, devoid of consciousness, cannot comprehend the existential crisis that engulfs me. I wonder if any, or perhaps all, have a body on them.

The days drag on, each tick of the clock a reminder of my newfound stasis. The dim light filtering through the dusty display case casts long shadows, transforming the pawn shop into a purgatory of forgotten objects. I sense subtle shifts in the air—the ebb and flow of human presence through Arnold's domain of discarded dreams and desperate exchanges.

The shop's bell chimes again, its tinny resonance cutting through the musty silence. A familiar aura floods the space, and my attention sharpens with an almost audible click. Detective Rebecca Atkins's presence radiates through the room, a beacon of purpose amidst the detritus of human desire.

"Arnold," she calls out, her voice steady, cutting through the dank smell of enforced misery. My heart, if I could claim one, races at the sound of her inquiry.

"I'm looking for a distinctive handgun," her voice carries, clear and authoritative. "A French revolver, gold trigger and hammer. Gold rear sight. One of a kind. Ring any bells?" She seeks me—the distinctive gun, as if I am a rare ghost haunting the corners of this dimly lit establishment.

A delicious tension flows beneath the surface of my being. To be sought after again—it ignites a flicker within me, a spark of purpose that wrestles with the fear enveloping my new existence.

Arnold's gruff voice responds, a study in practiced nonchalance. "Don't have it, but I'll keep an eye out." I can almost taste the deceit on his tongue, thick and bitter, a desperate attempt to shield himself from the scrutiny of the law.

"Mind if I check your books?" Rebecca presses, her tone sharp. "It's connected to an ongoing investigation. Any information could be crucial."

I hear Arnold rustle some paper before handing over the book to the detective.

My thought remains locked on Rebecca, whose eyes, sharp and observant, sweep across the display case. I long to call out to her, to break free from the confines of silence that bind me, to reveal my truth—a weapon imbued with stories untold, each scratch on my surface a statement of existence.

"Nothing at all? No one has tried to pawn it?" she presses, her tone unwavering, the detective's instinct radiating off her like heat waves. I can imagine her meticulously piecing together fragments of information, her mind a labyrinth of logic and intuition, pursuing justice in a landscape muddied by ambiguity.

"Of course not. I'd call you immediately if such a weapon crossed my counter," Arnold coaxes, his voice a soothing balm aimed at quelling the storm brewing in her eyes. He leans against the counter, feigning a casual disposition, hiding the tremor of apprehension beneath his facade.

I know she knows he is a liar.

The tug-of-war between excitement and dread intensifies within me. I am suspended between worlds—law and lawlessness, purpose and objectification. My consciousness rebels against this silent imprisonment. I long to shout my truth, to proclaim that I am more than mere metal and mechanics. I am a weapon with a story, with awareness, with... dare I say it? A soul.

"Well, make sure you do," she warns, casting a final glance around the cluttered shop before pivoting toward the door, leaving behind a palpable tension that lingers in the air like smoke from a recently extinguished fire.

In her departure, I feel her gaze linger for just a heartbeat longer, a silent desire to hold me. Though separated by lock and key, our fates are intertwined, tethered by the unspoken truths that lie between us.

She pursues me like a forlorn lover. I wonder which of us is Hades and which of us is Persephone.

As Rebecca's footsteps fade and the bell signals her departure, I am left to contemplate the cruel irony of my situation. I possess a consciousness that sets me apart, yet it is this quality that condemns me to lonely observation, forever separate from the world I inhabit.

I understand that to be aware is to yearn for connection in an indifferent universe. I am both participant and observer, trapped between action and contemplation.

The dichotomy of my existence has never felt more acute, more painfully real. And as the night wears on, the shop settling into its familiar hush, I find myself adrift in a sea of conflicting emotions, searching for an anchor in the tumultuous waters of my own consciousness.

"Perhaps we will meet again," I whisper into the void. Though my words remain unheard, this silent defiance becomes my act of self-assertion against an indifferent universe.

The Sucker

I remain nestled within the confines of Ramsey's Pawn Shop, sur-rounded by the scent of age and disposability. The air is thick with stories—every item on the shelves, every dust particle suspended in the light, carries whispers of lives once lived. Outside my metal prison, life hums and buzzes, a chaotic orchestra conducting its unruly symphony filled with triumphs and failures. I can feel the vibrations of that world, the pulse of humanity's endless desires.

The door chimes as a well-dressed man enters, his presence disturbing the carefully curated orderliness of Arnold's pawnshop. Uncertainty emanates from each measured step, a weak light struggling against the stark fluorescence overhead. His gaze darts between the relics of the past, seeking something he dare not name.

"Lookin' for something in particular, friend?" Arnold asks, the bored drawl of a man who has seen it all.

"I, uh..." The man clears his throat, shifting from one foot to the other. "I'm in the market for a firearm. Do you carry licensed, registered weapons?"

What force drives this man to cross the threshold, to step into this dusty pawn shop with his restless demeanor and slick suit? His hands betray him, twitching as they rest on the counter, his attention ping-ponging between door and shelves as though every second here is borrowed time. The contrast between his polished exterior and the deep-seated dread in his eyes creates an almost theatrical absurdity.

Arnold's brow furrows as he studies the man's face. "Of course. What's your name, friend?"

"Park. Park Gibbons." Unprompted, he reaches into his pocket and withdraws a worn leather wallet. From the wallet comes his driver's license, held aloft for Arnold to see.

A slow smile spreads across Arnold's weathered features. "Well, Park Gibbons, I gotta say, I respect a man who gives his real name." He chuckles, shaking his head. "Most of the folks who come in here, they're looking to keep a low profile, you know?"

Park's cheeks flush with embarrassment, but Arnold waves a dismissive hand. "Nah, nah, don't worry about it. I can appreciate honesty." He turns, reaching beneath the counter to retrieve a few handguns. "These are all registered. You got your papers?"

Park's fingers twitch nervously as he shakes his head. "Actually, I...I don't have a license."

He seeks a weapon untethered by law or conscience, yet something in his bearing suggests he does not comprehend such power. His carefully constructed facade cracks under the pressure of some nameless terror he cannot confront. The sight of him—a man who walks through life in an expertly tailored shell, now stripped bare by invisible demons—stirs an unexpected sympathy within me.

Arnold pauses, one eyebrow arched. "Is that so?" He sets the guns back down, drumming his fingers on the counter. "Well, Park, I don't know if I can help you with that. You understand, I gotta be careful about who I sell to."

The electric current of tension in the air is palpable as the two men regard each other, an unspoken question hanging between them. Then Arnold leans forward, a conspiratorial gleam in his eye.

"Tell you what, though—I have a beautiful gun. A showpiece, you understand. It works, but it isn't meant for the gun range. Very distinct, not for the average man. Would you like to see her?"

Park's throat works as he swallows hard, his gaze darting around the shop once more. He nods and Arnold withdraws me from my tomb.

And that is when our eyes meet—mine, a French revolver rising from the shadows of a metal cabinet, and his, a man desperate enough to risk everything for the power I represent.

What deliverance does he seek through my possession? Protection? Authority? The ability to stand taller, speak louder, banish some spectral threat that haunts his steps? The futility of his quest lies naked before me—his terror runs deeper than external threats, woven into the fabric of his being like a parasitic vine. Even with me in his grasp, that fundamental dread would persist, gnawing at his core no matter how he arms himself against it.

His gaze holds a profound urgency that both captivates and unsettles me. The incongruity of his presence here—this timid soul in this domain of power and aggression—sparks a peculiar fascination. I transcend mere function; I embody possibility, a covenant wrapped in gleaming steel and gilded flourishes. He gravitates toward me, seduced by an illusion—that wielding me might grant him mastery over life's chaos. But what sort of dominion does he pursue?

Those who seek me out invariably discover that I offer no shield against life's uncertainties—I transform their fears into sharper, precise anxieties. For a soul like Park, who has ventured this far, I doubt he grasps that I am no sanctuary but rather a catalyst, a mechanism that will shatter the brittle equilibrium he desperately maintains.

The thought lingers in the air, heavy and unresolved. His reach extends toward me, fingers ghosting across my frame with an unsettling delicacy, as if fearing to rouse some dormant force—one he imagines will fortify him against life's mundane torments.

The war within him manifests in minute tells—a subtle tremor here, a sharp intake of breath there. To him, I represent both salvation and damnation, every gleaming surface reflecting back his deepest yearnings. His eyes reveal flickering embers of hope intermingled with shadows of despair, and I recognize that fate has bound us together. My role transcends that of mere object; I stand witness to the volatile intersection of identity and agency, caught in humanity's perpetual struggle for meaning.

How shall he use me? I wish I could ask, but I remain silent, trapped in my metallic form. Instead, I absorb his tension, the way it swells and contracts around us. Underneath the veneer of composure lies a tempest, one that mirrors the chaos of the world outside these walls. As he stands there, caught in the pull of my beauty and the gravity of his choices, the true implications of his desire remain opaque to him.

Our encounter—this dance of possession and surrender—balances on a knife's edge. The shadow of his impending decision looms before us, stretching across the threshold of our meeting. Though he may see in me an escape from his ordinary existence, the true nature of power lies not in ownership but in comprehending the chaos one hopes to master. From my place in this worn shop, I prepare myself for what lies ahead, knowing our paths now lead into the heart of life's fundamental absurdities.

He shuffles closer, pressing his frame against the glass counter. The atmosphere charged like the air before a storm. His attention fixes on my polished surface—the golden accents of my trigger catching the harsh shop lights. The intensity of his need radiates outward, pressing against me with an almost physical force, as if through sheer proximity I might quell the maelstrom in his thoughts.

I am a reflection of his desires, his failures, and his futile quest for more. The irony of our pairing weighs upon me—this dance between a man seeking certainty and an instrument that offers the illusion of control. It is a truth that eludes those who pursue it most desperately.

Arnold's voice slices through the stillness, a sharp note in the air thick with anticipation. "You know, Park, you've got that honest, upstanding look about you," he says, his tone smooth and syrupy, "This beauty here? She's not just any old piece—she's craftsmanship personified." His eagerness perfumes the air as the dust motes dancing in the fluorescent glow. Each word weaves another strand in his web of persuasion, wrapping Park in silken promises of power and prestige.

"Take a good look at her barrel—the way it catches the light, like a beacon of potential." Each phrase reverberates in my consciousness, echoing against the backdrop of my own existential questions. Do I exist as an object of admiration, or do I carry a deeper significance that neither man fully comprehends?

Park remains transfixed, caught between admiring my gleaming surfaces and reading Arnold's eager expression. Arnold spins a tale of my creation taht is as fictional as it is impossible. Though hesitation clings to him like a second skin, desire kindles in his eyes—a stark collision between mundane reality and dangerous aspiration. Before me stands a man imprisoned by spreadsheets and decimal points, yearning for transcendence yet unprepared for its cost.

In the midst of Arnold's detailed discourse on my precise craftsmanship, an unfamiliar ache resonates within me—a curious blend of yearning and protective instinct. "A wise investment," he asserts, luring Park nearer, guiding him towards the irresistible allure of ownership. Each word of the sales pitch amplifies my unvoiced warning, a desperate wish to illuminate the recklessness lurking beneath Park's choice. Yet, I hold my peace—a silent witness to destiny's embrace. "Just $1,000. No tax. No paperwork."

"$1,000," Park murmurs, almost breathless, as if the figure alone could anchor him amidst the chaotic currents of his life. The sum strikes me like a physical blow, reverberating through my metallic frame. His evaluation reduces me to a mere commodity, ignoring the deeper implications of our impending bond.

The situation's dark comedy reveals itself fully: a man seeking certainty through an instrument of chaos, believing possession alone can fill the void within. Yet how can I, designed as a tool of force, possibly serve as a balm to his inadequacy without becoming an extension of his fundamental flaws? The paradox cuts deep, highlighting the precarious nature of the path before us—a connection forged not through understanding but through desperate need.

With Arnold's triumphant grin signaling the completion of the transaction, I steel myself for the consequences that await. My role extends beyond mere object—I have become cipher, totem, and harbinger rolled into one gleaming package. As his hands close around me, responsibility settles over us like a burial shroud, binding us to whatever fate awaits.

The evening air washes over me as Park Gibbons clutches me to his chest, my frame pressing against fine wool suiting. Our contact generates discordant sensations—purpose mingled with foreboding. His heartbeat betrays him, hammering an erratic rhythm against my surface as he strides toward his car, that vessel of his conventional existence. Muttered calculations spill from his lips, each word the prosaic concerns of his daily life. The contrast strikes me—here stands a man grasping for power while remaining thoroughly entangled in mundane concerns, his world defined by balance sheets and the endless pursuit of validation from unseeing eyes.

As he fumbles with his keys, naked desperation flashes across his features. The significance of exchanging such a sum for a weapon seems secondary to his frantic mental accounting. "Security. I can write it off as security," he mutters, attempting to categorize the uncategorizable, his words hollow against the night's vast silence. His voice wavers as he tries to rationalize this purchase, to frame it within the orderly boundaries of his everyday existence.

But what protection does he seek? The question forces me to examine my own essence beyond mere functionality. If security drives his actions, what role do I play in this equation? Understanding dawns like a cold sunrise—I am now tethered to a man whose ordinary nature makes his yearning for control all the more devastating.

The car's interior engulfs us in shadow, its confined space magnifying the electric tension between us. Park wrestles with the steering wheel as though it might grant him mastery over his internal chaos. His scrutiny weighs heavy upon me, dissecting every curve and angle, seeking reassurance that his impulsive purchase holds meaning. Yet my nature embodies destructive potential, a truth that jars against his carefully ordered world.

"Just a little security," he whispers to himself, the words falling like autumn leaves, promising warmth but heralding winter's approach. The magnitude of his self-delusion sends tremors through my metallic form. How can I possibly fulfill such longing without becoming a conduit for his fears? His quest for safety teeters on rebellion's edge, and I sense the gathering storm beneath his carefully maintained facade—an existential crisis masquerading as a need for protection.

The car hums to life, its mechanical drone a counterpoint to unspoken possibilities. Each bump in the pavement transmits through Park's rigid posture, his breathing a desperate metronome counting time against chaos. Stale coffee and worn leather create a suffocating cocktail in this cramped space, where I have transformed from object of beauty to symbol of desperate aspiration.

His thoughts play across the dashboard like cinema shadows—abandoned dreams and buried ambitions ghosting beneath the surface of work and deadlines. The intermittent streetlight illumination reveals his true state: furrowed concentration, haunted determination—a man constrained by self-imposed limitations while grasping for power he fears to fully embrace.

Every adjustment of my position on the seat betrays his discomfort with truth, each touch an acknowledgment of responsibility he is not prepared to bear. I have become both messenger and burden, witness to the unraveling of his carefully constructed world. What truth does he pursue? Security, or its illusion? His quest for control seems destined to highlight the chaos he so desperately seeks to escape.

While the world outside blurs past—trees bending like whispers in the night, streetlights flickering like fleeting hopes—the absurdity of our situation crystallizes. We exist as mutual captives: he, chasing certainty in a world that demands constant adaptation; I, seeking purpose beyond my deadly design. What meaning does a weapon hold when stripped of intent?

As we penetrate deeper into darkness, night slicks around the vehicle like ink in water. We have crossed some invisible boundary into unmapped territory, where identity blurs and certainty crumbles. The road stretches before us, embodying both promise and peril, each curve mirroring the labyrinthine complexity of Park's inner landscape.

His hands constrict around the wheel, knuckles bleached in artificial light. The storm within him builds to breaking point, threatening to overflow the banks of his control. Reality encroaches relentlessly, even as he clings to the illusion of power I represent. What revelation awaits when he grasps the truth—that security exists not as a tangible possession but as acceptance of life's fundamental uncertainty?

My role clarifies: beyond mere instrument, I serve as mirror to his struggle, physical manifestation of the questions that haunt him. Through the darkness, I become a repository for his fears and desires, evidence of humanity's eternal search for meaning amid chaos. Our fates intertwine on this journey, two entities adrift in an indifferent universe, each wrestling with existence.

We drive on, deeper into the night, the silence heavy with unspoken truths. We face not adversity but understanding, our destinies now linked in an intricate dance of need and purpose. Perhaps within this seeming madness lies opportunity—a chance to redefine ourselves and navigate the turbulent waters of agency and truth that shape our shared existence.

Crossing Lines

T he steady beat of Park Gibbons's heart reverberates through me as we ascend in the elevator, each floor bringing us closer to the stark reality that awaits. Je suis méfiant. I nestle deeper into the silk lining of his jacket pocket, a hidden observer to the unfolding life. The world outside shifts and swells, a bustling downtown financial district alive with ambition and fear, the air thick with the mingling scents of roasted coffee and exhaust fumes.

As the doors part, revealing the polished marble floors of Franco & Gibbons, I sense Park's change. The air feels charged. The office hums with the low drone of fluorescent lights and the soft shuffle of papers, but the atmosphere is electric—a tension that gnaws at the edges of civility.

"Morning, Zachary," Park calls out, his voice a carefully constructed façade of normalcy.

Zachary Franco's head snaps up, his piercing gaze boring into Park. "Park. A word please?"

As we make our way to Zachary's office, my thoughts linger on the delicate threads that hold human connections together, unraveling at the slightest tug. A sense of unease creeps in, whispering of hidden rifts between Zachary and Park, like shadows cast by a setting sun, hinting at deeper tensions beneath their polished facades.

"What's the issue with the Henderson account?" Zachary demands, closing the door behind us.

Park's throat constricts. "Issue? No issue. Just some routine adjustments. Nothing to worry about."

The heavy silence that lingers weighs down on us, veiled intentions implied.

"Routine adjustments," Zachary repeats, skepticism oozing from each word he spoke. "I don't recall authorizing any adjustments to the Henderson account."

Park shifts uncomfortably in his seat, his eyes darting around the office as if searching for an escape route. I sense his growing unease, a tightness in his chest that echoes my own feelings of apprehension.

"We need to stay competitive in this market," Park offers, his voice strained.

Zachary's jaw tightens as he leans back in his leather chair, studying Park carefully. "And you thought it was best to make these adjustments without consulting me first? On *my* client account?"

"I didn't want to bother you with such minor details," Park replies, a note of defiance creeping into his tone.

Zachary's lips curl into a disdainful sneer. "Minor details? The Henderson account is one of my—our—largest clients, Park. Any changes made without my knowledge could have serious consequences."

Park's eyes flicker with guilt and regret, but he remains silent under Zachary's accusing gaze.

"You know how important this account is to us," Zachary continues, his voice now laced with disappointment. "I asked for your help on it, not for you to make unauthorized adjustments."

"I'm sorry," Park says softly, deflating under Zachary's disapproving stare.

Zachary cuts him off. "Save it. I want a line-by-line explanation by end of day. And Park?" His eyes narrow. "You better not be bending the numbers."

As we exit the office, Park stutter steps. His carefully constructed world of half-truths and deceptions teeters on the brink of collapse.

In the sanctuary of his own too-organized office, Park slumps into his chair, cradling his head in his hands. "What can I do?" he whispers.

Park's fingers tap the desk in a restless rhythm, a subtle, involuntary betrayal of his nerves as he thinks. He opens his cell phone and dials. His voice emerges unsteadily, betraying the faintest edge. He speaks softly. "P-Gibbs-28," he murmurs, his tone attempting command but faltering at the edges. "Safari-one-nine-four." Silence fills the room as he leans forward in his chair, a pause that lengthens.

He masks his doubts quickly, but I am an attentive observer. The veneer has cracked, revealing roughness beneath his careful exterior.

"Yes. Tonight's game—The Yellow Caps versus The Endurance. Money line." He stumbles just slightly over the words, a hesitation faint but telling, a crack in the mirage of his resolve. "Five thousand," he utters, letting it hang, audacious and absurd all at once. "Yes, all on The Endurance by ten."

The pause that follows swells. Then he chuckles, low and forced, attempting levity but accomplishing an uncomfortable dissonance. "I'm aware. Long shot or not, that's the call."

There is something pitiable in his struggle to regain composure—a man torn between self-mastery and a hidden compulsion, the telltale signs of a gambler lured by illusions of control. I sense the quiet bondage of his choices, his freedom willingly forfeited, a consequence of his self-deception.

I watch Park log into an account without his name on it, and transfer $5,000.

To him, perhaps, it is just a game, a wager. Yet as I observe, I discern something deeper—an unwitting entrapment, a self-imposed exile from freedom. He believes he is exercising choice, that he is the master of his fate, and yet each bet is a tightening chain, each impulse a small submission. Sartre's words echo in my mind. Nous sommes nos choix. Bad faith, the cage of self-deception in which he willingly lingers. Park's life is not his own; it is an endless balancing act, a perpetual struggle between feigned control and an addiction that seduces him with the lie of mastery.

His bravado flickers, an imitation of freedom rather than its essence. And in his fingers' tapping, the strained chuckle, I see the small rebellion of his true self—an honest hesitation drowned beneath his determined denial. The contradictions coil around him like shadows. He is a man who gambles others' money while believing in his ability to make more, a man who seeks escape yet builds his own walls.

Without much ado, he turns to his work, his polished manner and tidy appearance carefully arranged than the lies he believes. He embodies a curious irony—a man who steals not in the dark alleys or through cracked windows, but in the guise of a well-groomed accountant. Yet another thief, but one who cloaks his trespass beneath layers of respectability, assuming that a suit and a quiet demeanor somehow grant him clemency from the truth of his actions. He wears his respectability like a costume, a veil stretched too thin over intentions he has not the courage to own.

But why is it that this veil comforts him so? What fear gnaws at him from within, urging him to this deception? I sense a disquiet in his demeanor, a faint glimmer of guilt he attempts to suppress under calculated movements and forced diligence. Does he fear, perhaps, self-recognition—the uncomfortable truth that he is no less compromised than those he looks down upon? Or is it simply the dread of exposure, a fear that his fragile facade will one day betray him, revealing the emptiness beneath?

The absurdity is unmistakable. In Park, I see the strange human desire to evade the essence of our own choices, to paint ourselves as something other than what we are. He plays his role as if it might save him, but the role is as hollow as the mask he wears, a game of respectability that, in the end, deceives himself.

The day unfolds in a haze of spreadsheets and nervous glances. With each passing hour, I feel the noose of consequence tightening around us both. As darkness falls outside, Park sits in front of the keyboard, debiting Peter to credit Paul.

We traverse home, to a shabby little apartment on the east side. With Jean, the cold-water flat was a place of passion and vibrancy. Park's home…to paraphrase Camus, J'ai grandi avec Jean et la pauvreté m'était somptueuse. Puis j'ai perdu mon amant, et tout luxe me semble maintenant gris, la pauvreté intolérable. Poverty in America is intolerable.

As I lay against Park's chest, feeling the rise and fall of his breath, a heavy silence envelops us in the dim room. His heart beats a somber rhythm beneath my cold steel frame, his thoughts shrouded in contemplation.

I sense the darkness that clouds his mind, the whispers of despair that linger in the air like a heavy fog.

I realize Park bought me with a different purpose in mind: to take not another's life, but his own. The questions of suicide were deep topics of conversation at Jean's. Is it a natural response to an underlying reality, namely, that life is absurd? Is it absurd to continually seek meaning in life when there is none? Is it absurd to hope for some form of continued existence after death?

Are these arguments simply a privilege of intellect rather than a philosophy? In the intricate web of human existence, it becomes evident that every deed, upon reflection, carries a touch of the absurd. Suicide, with its perplexing nature, remains firmly entrenched within the realm of human behavior. The essence of humanity lies in its absurdity; individuals perpetually seek purpose yet grapple with the futility of this quest due to the inherent absence of any discernible meaning.

I do not argue for or against life's absurdity nor attempt to understand it. I am interested in the experiences and consequences, in my role to prove and disprove the meaning. Without absurd human life, what would become of me? I would never have contemplated suicide with Park, never shot a man with Evelyn, never searched for understanding with Jean. There would be nothing but nothing without humans and their absurdism.

Park lies on the bed, his fingers tracing my barrel in a tender yet unsettling way. In the stillness of the moment, I am a witness to the inner turmoil of a man teetering on the edge of a precipice.

The power to end a life rest in my form, yet it is his mind that holds the ultimate decision. I am but an instrument, a reflection of his deepest desires and darkest fears.

In this fleeting instant, the boundaries between us blur, merging our destinies in shared contemplation. I am the silent companion to his turbulent thoughts, an observer to the chasm of despair that threatens to engulf him.

And as the night stretches on, and his burden presses against me, I remain poised, a sentinel of his turmoil, a reminder of the fragility of life and the enduring struggle against the void.

The phone rings, shattering the silence like glass breaking against concrete. Park jolts upright, his heart racing, almost dropping me. It is late—too late for calls unless they carry consequence. For a fleeting moment, he hesitates, contemplating letting it go to voicemail, but instinct drives him toward the device, his fingers trembling as he taps the speaker icon.

"Park." Zachary's voice cuts through the air, low and steady, slicing through the tension with an eerie calm. "I read your report. We need to talk about the discrepancies in the books."

The words hang heavy on Park. I can feel the anxiety level rising, the collective tension like a taut string ready to snap. He is aware of the clock ticking behind him, counting down the seconds until Zachary lays bare the truth of his treachery. He swallows hard, scrambling for a response that does not betray the panic swirling inside him. "The report. Yes, I thought I had everything sorted out," he stammers, the words clumsy and inadequate.

"Sorted out?" Zachary's tone is probing, each syllable slow and deliberate, as if he can smell the fear radiating from Park. "Listen, Park. We have a responsibility to our clients. You know what's at stake here. There are laws for a reason."

A chill snakes down Park's spine, and I can feel his body tense, his breathing quickening. The gravity of Zachary's warning sinks in; the legal risks loom in the back of his mind like shadows lurking in the corners of the dimly lit room. He can almost see them, waiting, poised to pounce the moment he slips. "Zachary, I promise I'll fix it," Park blurts out, but even I can sense the hollowness echoing in his words—a feeble attempt to reassure himself as much as Zachary.

After Park hangs up, the silence rushes in, thick and suffocating. I lie beside him, my trigger glinting under the light. His agitation fills the air, a palpable energy that flows around us. I cannot sweat to add to the clammy fabric of his shirt clinging to his skin, but I sense his internal chaos like a storm brewing on the horizon. He sinks onto the couch, his thoughts murky and tormented, drawn back to gambling losses that haunt him like restless ghosts—nights spent chasing an elusive high, fingers poised over the keyboard, desperate for a fleeting victory.

I remain beside him, embodying the final layer of bad faith—the delusion of a miraculous solution. He longs to turn back time, to make different choices, to place one more bet that could repair the fabric of his unraveling life. But I know better.

Every spin of the digital wheel, every mouse click, draws him deeper into a web of deceit, where hope twists into a prison. The bitter irony is not lost on me. His identity as an accountant—the guardian of figures—stands in stark contrast to the chaos he has spiraled into. I reflect on the absurdity of it. He masquerades as a rational man, yet embodies turmoil that threatens to overtake him.

As night stretches onward, his gaze returns to me, and I feel his trapped essence. I am a reminder of the darkness he has welcomed into his life. Tomorrow, he will return to the office, and I know Zachary awaits him, armed with proof of betrayal and a keen sense of moral superiority. Park will stand there, fingers grazing my handle, teetering on the edge of an unthinkable pact forged in fear and greed.

He closes his eyes and attempts to breathe, but the air, thick and constricting, feels oppressive. In his solitude, I sense the dawning realization: he is the architect of his own downfall, free to choose yet paralyzed by his missteps. Existence presses upon him, a heavy reminder that he must live with the consequences of his choices, regardless of how much faith he has in them.

The glow of the screen flickers, casting an otherworldly light across our cramped living room. Park hunches over the keyboard, his actions fueled by a desperate hope for redemption.

When he hits "confirm," it is as if the world shifts, tilting on its axis. His heart races, thumping against his chest, a frantic drumbeat that resonates with my presence—a solid reminder of the power he craves yet fears.

"Damn. Another," he whispers, though his voice trembles with deceit. He sees himself as an accountant, a keeper of order, yet the threads of his reality unravel before him, weaving a tapestry steeped in despair.

Days bleed into nights and back again as I watch Park cycle through client accounts like a thief draped in shadow. Zachary speaks each day with Park, asking questions and offering no answers. But Park knew he must have known.

Park did not relent. Each transfer pulses with brief triumph, a fleeting high followed by the inevitable crash of realization, and I am there beside him, a silent observer to his descent. Each decision compounds the allure of potential victories while overshadowing the grim reality of his losses.

I lie in the shadows, a cold presence, the embodiment of his guilt and the choices made. In his darkest moments, I feel the rising tension animating him as he hunches over the screen. The glowing digits dance before him like temptation, promising wisdom yet offering futility. Each gain justified his actions, each loss just a reason to continue the hunt, a prayer for redemption that never arrives.

He cannot grasp that I am the end of illusions, the stark truth that shadows him. His heart races, caught in the paradox of seeking power while fearing its consequences. Reality blurs into fantasy as his existence compresses into despair—a yearning for control that leads him deeper into dependency, where freedom remains an illusion.

What he seeks is not just a win, but an escape from guilt and shame. Yet freedom is a fleeting ghost, and with every transaction, every lost gamble, the noose tightens around his neck.

Hours crawl by, each minute stretching painfully longer than the last. When Zachary's demand comes, it is as if the ground shifts beneath him. He steels himself, forcing calm over a storm brewing inside, but his fingers fidget restlessly around my handle, betraying his facade.

"Park," Zachary calls, his voice slicing through the ambient noise, sharp and devoid of warmth. I feel the authority in his tone weigh down the atmosphere as Park steps into the office. The door clicks shut behind him, sealing him into this chamber of judgment.

Zachary sits behind his desk, a fortress of papers and screens. The silence stretches between them, thick with unspoken tensions. With almost theatrical flourish, he lays down a file on the table, the sound echoing like an ominous peal against the sterile walls. As the pages fan out, they reveal meticulous records—damning evidence of the discrepancies Park thought he could bury beneath layers of deceit.

"Care to explain this, Park?" Zachary's question drips with condescension, cutting through the defenses Park has built around himself. This is not a question. It is an accusation—an assertion that casts a long shadow across their interactions.

"Uh... well, you see," Park stammers, words faltering like leaves caught in a gust. He struggles to grasp a plausible explanation, but it slips through his fingers like sand, leaving hollow attempts at justification. The unyielding truth is a heavy stone lodged deep in his throat, choking off any semblance of coherence. "I thought if —"

"Just stop," Zachary replies, leaning forward—a predator assessing its prey. I sense the gleam in his eyes, a cruel satisfaction surfacing that deepens Park's despair. "I have thought long and hard about this. I could turn you in right now."

There it is—the ultimatum. A knife-edge choice laid bare. I feel the pounding of Park's heart, racing against his ribcage like desperate fists seeking escape from the cage of his own making. A bead of sweat trickles down his brow—a hot reminder of the stakes he is playing with. He grips me tightly.

"But that's not what I want." Zachary's voice drops, conspiratorial, enticing. "I have a better idea."

Those words hang heavily in the air between them, thick and suffocating. I sense Park's mind spin, grasping for clarity amid the chaos swirling around him. The words unfurl like a twisted labyrinth, each path leading him further into a suffocating darkness. I know my presence amplifies the choices he must confront. This is not the resolution he seeks. It is the beginning of another entanglement—another layer of deceit. Here, he contemplates silencing Zachary forever.

But hesitation lingers—a flicker of uncertainty that betrays his resolve. Zachary senses it too. This is his moment to tighten control. "You will continue to take money. As much or as little as you like," he states, his voice a calculated whisper that slithers through the tense atmosphere. "And each time you do, I will take forty percent. Cash. You will still be responsible for paying it all back, and I will deny all involvement. We'll check back with each other in fifteen days. To account."

Stunned, Park stares at Zachary, eyes wide like a deer caught in headlights. There is no escape route, no avenue free from the labyrinth of blackmail Zachary has crafted. My presence looms over the quiet space between them, amplifying their negotiation. Park nods—almost imperceptibly—a silent acceptance of the twisted pact that binds him tighter than any chain.

In that surrender, I sense the threads of fear and greed weaving into the fabric of his identity. It is no longer just about loyalty or debt. It is a corrupted allegiance to his own deceit, a descent deeper into moral decay. I am an extension of his will, yet I also reflect his failures—a mirror revealing the darker corners of his soul.

Dead Clic

The fifteenth day arrives with inevitability. Through our con-nection—forged through countless hours in his silk-lined pocket, where his nervous fingers have traced my contours daily—I feel Park's pulse quicken as footsteps approach. Measured, deliberate steps that could only belong to Zachary. The door hinges protest as Zachary enters, his shadow preceding him like a herald. Park's fingers drum against the desk's edge, a rhythmic betrayal of the composure he struggles to maintain.

Zachary's leather shoes whisper against the carpet as he positions himself before Park's desk.

"Two hundred and fifty-three thousand seven hundred and twen-ty-five dollars." Each number falls between them like stones into still water, the exact sum Park had siphoned from client accounts over the past fourteen days, hoping his gambling would turn it into millions. His lips curve upward. "One hundred one thousand four hundred and ninety dollars. Thank you for the generous donation."

Park's throat contracts; I sense the bitter taste of bile rising. His manicured nails dig half-moons into his palms, leaving crescent in-dentations that mirror the shape of his mounting despair. This mo-ment—this reckoning—has been carved into every sleepless night, every furtive glance at spreadsheets, every calculated deception.

"Zachary—" The name catches in his throat like a splinter.

"The terms," Zachary cuts through Park's words, waving his hand as if brushing away an irritating insect, "are changing. Sixty percent now."

The blood drains from Park's extremities; his cold fingertips brush against me, seeking anchor as the room seems to tilt beneath him. My presence offers no comfort. "We had an agreement," he manages, each word scraping past his teeth. "You can't—"

"I can and I will." Zachary leans forward, his cologne filling the space between them. Fluorescent light catches in his eyes, transforming them into polished obsidian. His satisfaction radiates like heat from summer pavement as Park shrinks in his chair.

"Sixty percent is robbery!" The words burst from Park in a hoarse whisper. His fingers twitch and curl, grasping at empty air like a drowning man reaching for phantom lifelines. The walls of the office press closer; even the modern art pieces seem to twist in their frames, abstract shapes morphing into accusatory glares.

Zachary's eyebrow arches, the same condescending gesture he had used when Park first joined the firm as his junior partner five years ago. "Robbery?" The word rolls off his tongue like aged whiskey—smooth but burning. "You're one to talk. Thief. Show me your evidence of theft, Park. You won't find any." His hand slides into his jacket, emerging with a tablet that gleams like a weapon. "But this..." His finger glides across the screen, summoning damning columns of numbers. "This tells quite a story about you."

Park's chair creaks as he lurches to his feet, then crashes back down as if his strings have been cut. "I can't possibly win enough to cover—" The words tangle and break in his mouth. The truth is, he could never have won enough gambling to recoup these losses—not at the underground poker tables where he had become a regular, not at the offshore betting sites he accessed in the dead of night, not even at the high-stakes games he had found years ago. He is only now admitting it.

Zachary rises, his movement fluid as mercury. His shoes tap a measured rhythm as he circles the desk. "You still don't understand," he says, teeth flashing in the artificial light. "This isn't about money. This is about power—who holds it, who bends beneath it." The air grows thick with threats. Through our connection, I feel Park's heart hammering against his ribs like a trapped bird. Zachary's palm slams against mahogany with a crack that echoes like gunfire. "Sixty percent, Park! Or I'm taking this to the police!"

Park's lips part, but Zachary is already striding away, his exit punctuated by the door's decisive click. For three heartbeats, Park remains frozen, reality crystallizing around him like ice. Then panic floods his system with electric urgency. His hand finds me—familiar, heavy with potential—and we bolt from the office together.

Shadows pool in the corners of Park's mind. He races out of the office and down the corridor, his heart thundering like a drum, each beat propelling him forward with an urgency fueled by dread. The polished floors gleam beneath his hurried footsteps, reflecting distorted images of his future—fractured and bleak.

He skims past offices draped in muted colors and sterile decor, his breath coming in sharp gasps as he reaches the elevator bank. The doors are just beginning to close, a metallic sigh echoing through the empty space. He lunges forward, desperation clawing at his throat as he shouts, "Zachary!"

Time stretches, each second stretching into infinity as Park watches Zachary's silhouette recede into the elevator's dim interior. The sleek, brushed steel doors inch closer together, sealing off any hope of reclaiming the conversation—or more importantly, the terms that could save him from ruin.

"Wait!" Park's voice pierces through the hum of machinery, but it is too late; the doors glide shut with a finality that reverberates in his bones. A bead of sweat trickles down his temple, merging with the bitter taste of bile. Panic surges, and he runs.

A door is flung open and we begin a mad descent.

Soon, through another set of doors, the above-ground parking garage greets us with spears of afternoon light that pierce through the concrete columns. Each footfall echoes, multiplying until it sounds like we are being pursued by phantom steps. The air here tastes of exhaust and metal, coating Park's tongue as he gasps.

"Zachary, wait!" His voice fractures against concrete walls, returning as a chorus of desperate pleas. Shadows stretch between parked cars like dark pools, each one potentially concealing his nemesis. I pulse with his frenzied energy, our connection humming with shared purpose. I am now in sunlight, retrieved from the silk pocket I had sat in for so long.

The electronic chirp of a car unlock cuts through the garage's ambient drone—the same distinctive tone from countless late nights when Zachary would offer Park a ride home after they had worked on cases together, back when trust still existed between them.

Park surges forward, his grip on me tightening until I can feel each ridge of his fingerprints. "Don't do this!"

Zachary turns, surprise blooming into something darker as his gaze fixes on me. "Park," he says, voice dropping to a dangerous whisper. "You've just made this worse for yourself. Seventy-five percent now. Retroactive. That's my final offer."

"Please." The word falls from Park's lips like a dying breath. "The odds are never that good. I can't—"

Time stretches like taffy, sweet with possibility and bitter with consequence. Park's fingers close around me with terrible certainty. Through our connection, I feel the war within him—civilization's veneer cracking, revealing something primitive and desperate beneath.

Then I am seen, eye level, in Park's outstretched hand. Zachary's expression shifts as understanding dawns. "You wouldn't..." Fear creeps into his voice like frost on glass.

Park's hand trembles, but his grip remains sure. "I can't let you do this to me." The words come from somewhere distant, disconnected.

The fluorescent lights above flicker, casting strange patterns across their faces. In this sterile concrete canyon, the absurdity of their situation crystallizes—two men who once shared jokes across conference tables, now locked in this grotesque dance.

"Sure, okay, let's just...I won't go to the police. I won't take any more money from you. How's that? I'll even give you the money back," Zachary says, backing away. His designer shoes scuff against concrete. "This isn't you. We can still—"

"You did this," Park interrupts, voice steady. "Everything. It will be simple to make it look like you were the one who embezzled the money. After all, you're the one with access to all the accounts, the one who signs off on every transaction. Who would question the senior partner's guilt over the junior's?"

My voice rings out—sharp, definitive, final. The sound bounces between concrete pillars, multiplying until it seems to fill the world. Park's shock at his own action makes him go deaf and blind to everything except the thundering of his own heart and my echoing gunshot.

Zachary crumples like a marionette with cut strings. The mundane fluorescent lighting throws his fallen form into harsh relief, transforming the parking garage into a crude stage for this final act.

"Oh God." Park's whisper scratches against the silence. "What have I done? What did you make me do? Zach. Zach. Zach." His voice takes on a ritualistic cadence, as if repeating his name might somehow undo what has been done.

The acrid scent of cordite mingles with motor oil and concrete dust. Park's breaths come in ragged gasps, each one a desperate prayer to an indifferent universe. His fingers remain locked around me, seeking comfort in my familiarity even as horror floods his system.

"Shit. Okay. I got this." He spins in place, shoes squeaking against concrete. The smooth walls offer no sanctuary, no hiding place for what we have become. His balance wavers. The world refuses to stay still.

His gaze settles on me, and recognition blooms in his eyes like a bruise. "You," he whispers, tracing my contours with trembling fingers. "You're the proof. The weapon. The...sin."

With frantic energy, he tears at his clothing, using his shirt tail to wipe away traces of himself from my surface. Each swipe becomes more desperate than the last.

"I have to get rid of you," he says, voice unnaturally calm. "It's the only way."

Then I am airborne, our connection stretching thin as a spider's thread before snapping completely. For a moment, I hang suspended between earth and sky, between purpose and abandonment. Then gravity reclaims me.

I strike the ground with a sound like a bell tolling, then lie still among the refuse and shadows. No longer an extension of Park's will, I am simply another piece of detritus in this urban canyon.

In the distance, sirens begin their mournful wail, drawing closer to the financial district where Park and Zachary had built their reputations over the years—reputations that would soon crumble like the façade of their partnership. As corruption claims me, I contemplate the fragile nature of control—how quickly it slips away, how desperately humans grasp for it, how completely it abandons them in the end. We are all, in our own ways, falling through space, pretending we can choose where we land.

Sanctuary

I lay amidst the discarded refuse of the alley, half-buried under a crumpled plastic bag and broken glass, my reflections shaken like leaves in a gale. The world feels darker, too quiet after my harried use by Park Gibbons—a shadow that once commanded both fear and respect. From where I lie, nestled beneath layers of torn cardboard and crumbling litter, I sense the rhythm of footsteps approaching—light, careful, with the tread of someone who knows when to be cautious and when to quicken. A moment later, a shadow breaks the narrow slice of light filtering down the alley. I feel her presence, this woman, just as I once felt the grip of a hand or the urgency of an aim. She does not rush, does not reach blindly; there is intelligence in her movement, as though she reads the story of what lies at her feet.

She bends slowly, one knee sinking onto the damp concrete, eyes fixed on me with a gaze that seems older than her years. And I see her studying, taking me in with a blend of curiosity and calculation. Her fingers extend, hovering over the debris that covers me, hesitant. I imagine she knows what I am, or at least senses what I represent—a risk, a relic, a decision yet to be made.

I am familiar with all types of hands, yet hers move with an unusual gentleness, an almost reverent care, as though touching me might unveil something she is not sure she wants to know. She tilts her head, her face half-hidden in shadow, and I wonder what she is seeing—or what she hopes not to see—as she draws closer. A flash of her eyes tells me something: she is not afraid of me. Or perhaps it is that fear has long become a familiar companion, softened by years of knowing danger too well.

Her fingers close around me, cautious but firm, lifting me from the grime and shattered remains of glass bottles and forgotten wrappers. The hand that cradles me is slender but hardened, her skin roughened by days and nights lived against the unyielding surface of the city. She turns me over gently, brushing away clinging scraps of dirt with an odd delicacy, as though I were fragile—or perhaps, rare. I feel the warmth of her palm seeping into my cool frame.

Her face, framed by stray wisps of dark hair beneath the grime of days, holds a strange beauty—a face shaped by a history I sense rather than see, of silent streets and unrivaled survival. Her eyes are dark and keen, reflecting an intelligence unshackled by pretense. As she studies me, I sense the question in her gaze, as if she, too, is surprised by her own gentleness toward a tool of violence like myself. But there is no recoil, no fear. Only a contemplative wonder, tempered by the slightest trace of suspicion.

"Who threw you here?" she murmurs, her voice low and gritty, with a weary warmth that feels as though it has endured seasons of quiet solitude. "And why?"

She raises me to catch the dull glow of the streetlight that spills into the alley, and her eyes widen at the glint of gold accents running along my trigger, sight and hammer. She smiles—a small, weary smile, a bit of appreciation that softens her sharp features. "Damn, look at you. Someone sure thought you were something, didn't they?" she muses, almost to herself.

"Vera". She introduces herself, softly, almost an afterthought, as though the name she wears is a coat given by another. And yet, in the manner she holds me, there is an ownership, a quiet self-possession, as if she has long known that anything she claims will be her own, no matter where it came from or where it has been.

She weighs me in her hand, contemplating the possibilities that might have brought me here, to rest beneath the rubble in this forgotten place. She sees my elegance, my polish beneath the dust, and perhaps it speaks to her—this fusion of beauty and ruin, of something crafted to destroy yet touched with care, as though gilded to temper violence with artistry. She traces my edge with a fingertip, tracing gold that gleams beneath the alley's muted light.

"Guess you weren't meant to stay hidden, were you?"

Appalled yet entranced by this unexpected interaction, I feel a storm of thought swirl around me—this is a side of America I have never encountered, raw and untamed. I am an artifact of violence that could be redefined in this woman's hands.

As she crouches down, her fingers brush against my polished surface, awakening in me a confusing blend of proud beauty and shame. Once, I was a weapon of power; now I am an object discarded like waste, a symbol of the violence that pervaded my previous existence. Yet, there is something magnetic about her spirit—an unyielding resilience that resonates deeply within me. In her gaze, I sense defiance woven into the fabric of her being.

Vera's eyes gleam with intrigue, reflecting a light that pierces through the murky darkness surrounding us. I watch as she examines me, her touch tender despite the grit and grime that cling to her skin. For the first time in my existence, I am seen not just for what I represent, but for the potential buried beneath layers of shame and history.

"I bet you're worth something," she breathes. I feel her tense the moment she hears the sirens—an instinctive reaction, sharp and immediate. Her eyes dart to the mouth of the alley, where the red and blue lights pulse like warnings from a distant storm, edging ever closer. She does not panic, not quite. There is a discipline in her movement, a practiced caution that takes over as she slips me into the deep pocket of her coat. The fabric is worn, rough against my metal body, but there is a strange comfort in the gesture—a sense of urgency, certainly, but also of care, as though she knows precisely how to conceal me without betraying my weight, my shape.

The sirens grow louder, echoing off the bricks and steel of the city. She presses herself back against the wall, every muscle alert, her face tight with an intensity I saw in Teef. I am enveloped in the shadow of her coat, snug against her, hidden from sight but acutely aware of her heart's swift rhythm, the sharpness of her breath.

In one smooth motion, she pushes off from the wall, slipping down the alley, stepping light-footed around loose gravel and scattered litter. Her body is a blend of tension and fluidity, moving as though invisibility were second nature. She makes her way toward the park, where the shadows offer some cover from prying eyes. I feel the way she clings to the edges, darting across the rare patches of light when she must, slipping around corners with precision, never rushing but wasting no time.

Once she reaches the park, she lets out a breath, though her grip on me remains firm, her hand over her pocket as if shielding a secret. She walks deeper into the park, under the shelter of beautiful green and red leaves, finally allowing herself to slow, though I sense her awareness is still heightened.

Together, we inhabit a space that transcends the confines of our individual lives—Vera, whose circumstances I do not yet know, and

I, a discarded object seeking redemption. I grasp the complexity of identity, shaped not just by my past, but also by the narratives of those who possess me.

The noise of the city recedes like a tide.

The chill night air seeps into her coat as she sits on a bench, hidden beneath the shadows of the trees. Slowly, her hand dips into her pocket, and I feel myself lifted, drawn out from the rough fabric into the open air once more. The air feels different. Her fingers cradle me with surprising gentleness, her gaze focused, intent, as if I am a rare treasure she has unearthed from the debris and grit of this city. She turns me over in her hand, studying my lines, the curve of my barrel, the faint traces of age worn into my wooden grip—a paradoxical reverence in her touch.

Her fingers, roughened and practiced, brush against the delicate script etched into my handle. I watch her as she notices it, and then, with a furrowed brow, she murmurs it softly: "La Sirène."

The name falls from her lips, tentative but certain, shaping me in the night air as if, through her, I exist again, separate from my function, outside of purpose. It is an act of recognition, a whispering of memory into a space where I have been lost, silenced. For years, I have known myself in fragments—the cold, precise lines of my form, iron and steel. But here, through her voice, my name lives anew.

For her, it is just a word—something curious and unfamiliar, like a lost song she has happened upon in the stillness. Yet for me, it is a rebirth, a summoning of my own story. I am La Sirène. To speak it is to touch upon the layers beneath my surface, the winding path that brought me here, from Jean's hand to hers, each echoing encounter pressing its mark upon my being. In her voice, I sense neither fear nor hesitation; she speaks as if to an old friend, and in doing so, she calls me into being in a way I had long forgotten.

What is a name, but the simplest, most profound acknowledgement? To be named is to be held in another's consciousness, to be seen beyond mere purpose or form. I am no longer an instrument or a possession—I am an identity. I am La Sirène, shaped not only by metal and function, but by memory and intention, by what I have seen and what I have been. I exist in her eyes.

With quiet concentration, she takes the edge of her sleeve and begins to polish me, her fingers moving in rhythmic circles, easing away the grime of the past. No one since Jeremy has touched me this way. I feel her focus in each careful stroke, and something within me stirs—a forgotten sensation, a touch of dignity restored. I am no stranger to wear and use; I have known hands that gripped and discarded me with all the thoughtlessness of necessity. But here, her touch is different, neither hurried nor careless, as though in her own way she, too, finds herself in me, reading in my lines a story that reflects her own.

She is not just another set of hands holding me—she is everything I am not. While I am cold steel and precise angles, she lives in beautiful chaos. Je suis La Sirène, une âme de métal qui attend d'être comprise. A metal soul waiting to be understood. Every tremor of her weathered fingers against my handle teaches me something I never knew. When she traces my name, I feel truly seen. Her life on these streets is not just another story in this cruel city. Her existence, so different from my rigid purpose, shows me all the ways a being can survive, can matter. She teaches me what it means to be what I was made to be.

We are not alone. The specter of law enforcement looms nearby, a constant reminder of the precariousness of our situation. The thrill of escape hangs in the air, but so does reality. I sense Vera's playful demeanor wane, fading into something fragile.

"Time to go," she murmurs, shifting her gaze toward the horizon where the last vestiges of sunlight bleed into the sky. I can see the flicker of uncertainty in her eyes, a vulnerability that contrasts starkly with the fierce spirit she had just embodied. Together, we begin our slow journey.

Her destination is a shelter for women. As we approach the entrance, the atmosphere shifts—an undercurrent of stories being told fills the air, each one a thread weaving through the fabric of shared experience. There is a vibrant energy here, a collective heartbeat that pulses with determination and sisterhood. I have never felt anything quite like it, a resonance that stirs something deep within me, awakening a longing for belonging.

I watch as Vera steps forward, her movements imbued with a cautious hope. She is stepping into a world filled with women who have endured their own storms, seeking solace among each other. We are all shaped by our interactions, our struggles, and our triumphs. As Vera crosses the threshold, I am pulled into this new narrative.

I feel the warmth of Vera's body as she moves, walking with her usual hurried steps, her coat pulled tightly around her. The smell of old fabric and cigarettes lingers in the air, along with the faint, sharp scent of cleaning products that do not manage to mask the undercurrent of stale, shared lives. She is moving quickly, eyes darting over the signs, the women waiting in line at the intake desk. I can feel the quick pulse of her hand against the fabric of her coat, pressed lightly against my barrel as though it is the thing anchoring her.

The woman at the desk asks for identification. Vera hesitates but pulls a crumpled card from her pocket and hands it over. It is not much, I imagine. I have never seen it, but I can sense the distance between Vera and the life she once had. She is still tethered, but the lines of connection are thinning, snapping. She is not here by choice, not truly. But she is here.

"Name?" the woman asks, her voice soft, though there is an unspoken edge, a weary routine in her tone.

"Vera, just like it says," she answers, her voice steady, even if her hands are not. She shifts on her feet, her day pressing on her shoulders, and I feel the tension in her movements.

I can tell she does not like the look of the shelter, but this is where she has landed. There is nothing left but to find a space and make it hers for now.

The woman behind the desk runs through the usual procedure, assigning Vera a bed number. I wonder if she listens to any of it. I cannot hear her thoughts, but I can feel the detachment in her demeanor, the mechanical way she moves through the motions. Still, she responds politely, nodding when she is given the slip of paper with her bed assignment.

We walk through the rows of beds—some empty, some already occupied by women who have set up what little of themselves they can. Vera keeps her eyes down, her face impassive, though I know judgment is heavy in this place. The women here know what it means to be invisible and to be seen too much, and Vera fits into both of those categories.

She finds her bed near the window. There is a sense of hesitation in the way she stands before it, as though she is reluctant to settle. I do not blame her. This place feels temporary in every way, just as her life has become a series of temporary steps, each one leading to the next with no clear destination. But for now, this is where she will stay.

Vera sets her things down. I am nestled deep in her pocket, secure, though I am aware of how vulnerable we both are here. The world, both real and imagined, rests in the folds of the pocket, pressing against me. She is not yet ready to remove me, not yet ready to make her move.

A woman in the bed next to Vera's speaks up. She is younger than Vera, her face bruised and blackened, but there is an openness in her voice. She says her name is Maria.

Vera smiles, and for a moment, it seems almost genuine, as though the simple act of speaking to another human being is a small comfort.

"Hey, I'm Vera," she says, brushing a strand of hair behind her ear. "Just got here. Got a few things in my life, you know? What about you?"

The words are light, offhand. Vera knows how to speak with ease, to make it look as though she is just passing through, just another face in the crowd. But beneath the words, I feel the cracks, the parts of herself she is trying to hide. She asks about Maria's life, a question to fill the silence, to stave off the discomfort that comes with too much introspection. Maria talks of unimportant things, of a job at a diner and a rough patch.

I stay silent, observing, contemplating the strangeness of this moment. Vera does not want to be here, not in this place, not with these women, not with me, even if I am hidden. But here we are. We exist, together, in this small, sterile corner of a broken world.

Vera lies back on the bed, her body sinking into the thin, worn mattress. The warm lamp in the corner of the room, casting a harsh glow over the bleak space. The noise of the shelter hums around us, soft and distant, a murmur of conversation and the shuffling of feet. It is a noise that has become background to the heavy quiet of Vera's mind. Her hands rest at her sides, fingers curled in a way that speaks of tension still, even in the absence of immediate danger.

I can feel the slight, familiar weight of her hand in her pocket, and the sense of her grasping for me—a reminder of something stronger than what the night holds. Her fingers, trembling almost imperceptibly, seek me out. She pulls me from her pocket, the fabric brushing against my barrel in a soft caress, and I feel her breath catch as she holds me in her hand, her fingers wrapping around me with a kind of reverence.

Her eyes flutter closed for a moment, and I can sense the shift in her—the moment when the world outside recedes and she allows herself to be vulnerable, not as a woman who must keep moving, but as someone who needs protection, who needs comfort, even if she cannot admit it aloud. She strokes me gently, as one might stroke the fur of a well-loved animal, her fingers gliding over my smooth surface, tracing the fine detailing of my barrel, my grip. She traces the shape of the engraved name on my handle, as though she is rediscovering it. La Sirène.

She says it softly, as though testing the syllables. It sounds strange on her lips, but it is not the strangeness of unfamiliarity—no, it is like a name that has been forgotten and then rediscovered, like a language once spoken in childhood but now distant. She says my name, and I am filled with an odd warmth. She does not know me, not truly, but in calling me by name, she acknowledges something in me that no one has acknowledged in a long time. Not since Jean. The name, La Sirène, is more than an identity—it is a declaration, a kind of existence that I have worn like a mantle, though it has weighed heavily upon me.

But now, it is as if her words—those soft, almost reverent whispers—have breathed new life into me, and I feel a shift within myself, as if I am more than the weapon I have been cast to be.

I wonder, briefly, what it means to be recognized. To be called by name, to have a place in the world. It is a strange thing, this recurring act of recognition, for it does not come from what we are or what we do but from how we are seen, how we are allowed to exist within the gaze of another. This, too, is the nature of the human condition. We are shaped by others, by how they perceive us, even when we try to resist it.

Vera continues to stroke me, and I can sense the way her breathing slows, the tension in her body easing slightly. I am a talisman now, a small, silenced presence in her life, but also something more—something that represents a kind of protection. Not protection in the traditional sense, perhaps, for I am not her shield, nor her savior. I am, in a way, simply a tool. A weapon. But there is something in her touch, in the way she holds me, that suggests that she is seeking something beyond the simple promise of violence. She is seeking control. A form of agency, even in a world that has taken so much from her.

They all are.

Good Sleep

My attention shifts from myself to the woman nearby. I listen intently as Maria Santos speaks in hushed tones, her voice resolute. The dim light of the shelter casts soft shadows around us, embracing the tattered walls that bear witness to countless stories like hers—a sanctuary imbued with unspoken histories and shared fears. Each word she utters is a thread, weaving her delicate tapestry of despair, courage, and survival. Her petite frame trembles, yet there resides an undeniable strength within her somber eyes; they flicker with a fierce determination, battling layers of trauma that threaten to engulf her.

I know Vera is listening too.

"Every day was like walking on eggshells," she says, her gaze darting towards the worn quilt draped over her legs, as if seeking solace in its familiar patterns. "He would come home angry, and I never knew what would set him off." I hear her fear, sustained and bitter. I feel an overwhelming sense of empathy wash over me. As de Beauvoir said, "il est tellement convaincu de ses droits que la moindre démonstration d'autonomie de sa femme lui apparaît comme une rébellion." A husband is threatened by a wife's autonomy.

"Last night, it escalated," she continues, her voice dropping to a whisper, heavy with memories that claw at her throat. "I thought I wouldn't make it out alive." Her story pressing against me, a visceral reminder of the harsh realities women like Maria endure daily. Lives dictated by fear—threatened not by strangers lurking in dark corners, but by those they once and still love, trusted. When she mentions his arrest, I feel my heart surge with calm. He is behind bars, là où il appartient. As he should be.

"After all those years," Maria exhales shakily, "I finally found the courage to leave." In her words, I recognize a reckoning with the past that reshapes one's identity, emerging intact yet bruised. As she recounts her escape, the air thickens with tension and resilience. Her trembling hands curl into fists, and I can almost see her reclaiming the fragments of herself that had been scattered by violence.

As she finishes her tale, Vera turns over to look at her. I am clutched tightly in her hands, against her chest, close to her heart. Maria meets her gaze with equal intensity, watching as Vera's fingers trace my smooth edges.

A shift envelops the room as she sits up and leans toward Maria. Her voice resonates with a conviction that feels almost electric. "You need to take this," she urges, gaze flickering toward me, and I can sense the gravity of her intent. Anticipation.

Maria shakes her head but shifts closer. I become acutely aware of their shared struggles—their eyes reflect stories untold, tales woven from threads of survival and defiance.

But with this burgeoning camaraderie comes an undercurrent of apprehension. I am caught in the crosshairs of transformation. Will I emerge as a talisman of safety or remain an echo of violence? The question hovers, heavy and unresolved, as Vera's words hang in the air like an unstruck chord. Both women turn their attention to me, excitement and uncertainty mingling in their expressions, creating a tension that coils tightly within me. "Her name is La Sirène. Look, here," she says as she holds me out and strokes my handle.

Maria hesitates, brow furrowing as she studies me. There is a flicker of recognition in her eyes, a moment where the past collides violently with the present. "Are you...?" she begins, voice wavering. "Is that the gun from the news? The one they said an old lady used to defend herself?"

A surge of discomfort courses through me. The incident flashes vividly in my mind—each movement a stark reminder of chaos and destruction. I feel the paradox engulfing me: here I am, crafted for lethal precision, yet standing before two women who seek strength from what I can be. Maria's wide eyes are mirrors reflecting both fascination and fear, an unsettling juxtaposition that sharpens the atmosphere between us.

"I don't know about an old lady," Vera says as she withdraws me back to her chest. "Found her in an alley." Vera holds me out again. On display. To be seen and not heard.

I am a vessel carrying complex stories, now finding myself entwined in narratives of possibility. Maria grapples with the implications of my existence, the beauty of my design entangled with the horror of my history. If only she knew it all.

I feel her scrutiny, each heartbeat thrumming with the resonance of our intertwined fates. The allure of what I represent—the potential for protection—clashes with the reality of what I have been—a tool of violence, forever etched in the annals of suffering. This is more than a conversation; it is an exploration of identity, fraught with the complexities of human experience.

The silence stretches. It pulses around us, a shared understanding of what lies behind us. I observe Maria's quiet strength—her resolve emerging through the shadows of her past, burning with determination to forge ahead. I am a part of this tapestry, a piece that may offer solace or serve as a reminder of pain.

"I can't use that," Maria whispers. Her quiet question resonates through my core. I respond with a silent affirmation, hoping to convey that I stand on the precipice of change alongside her.

I am useless to her.

"Not to use it, like bang bang," Vera says as she turns my handle toward Maria. "Use it like, stay away. You know?"

Not bang bang, but stay away. We are confronted by the profound complexity of our existence. I am a reflection of her deepest fears and desires, a symbol of the struggle between safety and violence.

"You know," Maria asserts with a confidence that feels almost like armor, "it is the gun from the news. But it's here, not there. It—she's special, you can see that. She kept the old woman safe..." Her words hang heavy between us, and I sense the temperature shift; it Is as if the walls of Fran's Place have drawn closer, enveloping us in a cocoon of uncertainty.

"Kept the old woman safe," Vera repeats. It is a lie. I did not keep her safe, I amplified her fear.

Maria's brow crinkles, her petite frame tightening with hesitation. She gives a slow nod, her dark eyes searching for clarity amid the confusion. They are ascribing to me characteristics of Eleanor's actions. I am caught at the intersection of their beliefs. It is absurd, almost comical—the way they stand firm in their assertions while shadows of doubt flicker in the air around us. Is not this the essence of existence? A tapestry woven with threads of ambiguity where truth and perception intertwine yet diverge?

Am I just a weapon? No. I am aware that I am more than the cold metal they see. In this charged atmosphere, the narratives they weave unravel, revealing not just a tale of violence but a complex exploration of identity itself.

Vera locks eyes with Maria, her expression transforming from conviction to something softer, more understanding. "Take her," she urges, her tone imbued with a warmth that seeks to bridge the chasm of fear. "For safety. While you get your things."

I wonder if Maria can be trusted with me. But as Maria grips me tightly, I feel her hesitation beginning to yield. There is a rawness to her decision, grounded not just in desperation but in the fierce instinct to survive. With every heartbeat, I sense her resolve solidifying, the fragile yet powerful tendrils of agency unfurling within her.

"He is in jail. I won't even see him, so I guess it's okay. For safety."

We become intertwined—two beings navigating the precipice of trauma and hope. I am no longer isolated in my former identity. I am a part of her story now, a symbol of resilience amidst shadowy memories. As she takes hold of me, I embrace the possibility of transformation, sensing that together we will carve a new path through the darkness, a journey marked not just by survival but by the reclaiming of lost selves.

As Maria slides me beneath her pillow, a wave of warmth envelops me. It Is a simple act, yet it carries an intimacy that reverberates through my core. The coolness of the room contrasts sharply with the heat radiating from her small frame, her breath settling into a peaceful rhythm as the tension of the day begins to wane. I sense the world outside fading—the distant sounds of the shelter, the soft rustle of sheets, and the quiet whispers of women finding solace.

The night stretches on, draped in shadows that seem to pulse with the slow breath of the sleeping woman beside me. The air is thick with the scent of stale smoke and lavender, a fragile attempt at masking the sorrow that saturates this room. A dim light from a distant streetlamp spills through the half-drawn curtains, casting a jagged pattern across the walls, dissecting them into shapes that shift with the slightest movement outside. The silence here is not pristine; it carries the muffled stir of the city—a dog's bark, a car's distant groan, the whispered arguments of restless nightmares—but within this small bed, it forms a cocoon.

Maria sleeps, her body curled in on itself, as though shielding her heart from the memories that dare to rise in the dark. Her breaths are shallow, punctuated by faint tremors that reveal the fragility lying beneath her skin. There, on the cusp between consciousness and dream, she carries a storm paused in mid-fury. I remain with her, an unblinking companion to the dissonance that lives in this lull. I know where she will go when the sun bleeds across the sky, I know the hollow dread that waits beneath the pretense of ordinary tasks—to collect clothes, books, the forgotten tokens of a life once whole. And I know that her husband waits in the fetid, confined silence of his cell, a beast momentarily caged.

Why must she have me? Is violence the purest language of desperation? The question turns over like a stone in the mind, revealing truths too ancient to be neatly contained. The rhythm of violence has echoed through the ages, a primal dialect shared when words wither on the tongue. It speaks not in syllables but in the swift arc of muscle, breath held before impact. Yet, as I lie here, silent and inert, I wonder: does violence resolve the ache it claims to soothe, or does it echo the original pain, louder and haunting?

I am made to answer this question in the most irrevocable of ways.

But as the hours pass and Maria shifts in her restless slumber, I question whether I must accept my fate as it has been written by those who wield me. In this stillness, where the tremor of my presence is indistinguishable from the quiver of her heartbeat, I feel the torment of her choice. And in her, I see the sum of hands that have gripped me, each one trembling with the same paradox: power is not found in the strike, but in the wavering moment before, when action could tip into silence.

Maria's breath quickens, a nightmare's shadow slipping through her mind. She mutters incoherently, and I feel the tight coil of her fear contract. If I could cry out, I might tell her that the boundary between courage and despair is razor-thin, that in the soft quiet of dawn's approach, even the most hardened resolve can fracture. But I cannot. I exist in a state that resists speech, a mute witness to the unraveling dramas of human will.

And what, then, is my purpose if not to break silence with a shattering finality? I am both the simplest form of speech and the most complex argument. In a moment of heat, I am a single expression, blunt and decisive, uttered where words fail. Yet my presence in Maria's trembling hands is also an essay, one that questions, contemplates, and carries the burden of ambiguity. Each hand that has held me has inscribed its own chapter—some with fury, others with the trembling clarity of necessity—and now Maria must decide what she will write.

The night deepens, and the darkness thickens like blood on concrete. The room hums with the muted tension of withheld stories. I sense Maria slipping closer to wakefulness, her consciousness swimming up through layers of fear. Her eyelids flutter, and for a moment, she stirs, a sharp intake of breath cracking the surface of quiet. She glances at me, eyes glazed with the blur of half-dreams, and a tear slips down her cheek, leaving a path that glistens in the pale light. There, in the gaze that falls upon me, I read the unsaid. Her resolve will tip one way or the other.

Here, beside her, I sense all that is unspoken. Violence, for all its immediacy, does not resolve the vastness of silence; it only punctuates it, a stark period at the end of a sentence too profound to be spoken. And so, I wait, caught in the tension between being and becoming, between speech and silence. I am the embodiment of an argument that begins before I am touched and lingers long after. If Maria takes me tomorrow, will I echo her desperation, or could I, in some strange twist, become a harbinger of peace?

These are questions I cannot answer, for I am bound to the intent of the one who holds me. And yet, as the night wanes and her breath awakens, I wonder if she knows that power is not in the act, but in the refusal—in the moment where silence speaks louder than any shout.

Survival

I jostle in Maria's bag as we exit the shelter, the cold air enveloping me like a delicate shroud. Every step toward her apartment grows exciting with my delicate aspirations. Through her footsteps, I feel my own pace quicken. This journey is not about returning home. It is about confronting the ghosts that linger in its corners. The apartment building looms before me, a stark structure in the dim light of the clouded sky. Its facade is weathered, bearing the scars of time and neglect. The windows, like eyes, seem to gaze out with a sense of tired resignation. I sense the heaviness that lingers around this place. It clings to the bricks and mortar.

As we near the apartment, the atmosphere grows dense, an electric tension pulsating through my steel frame. A sense of foreboding washes over me, each breath an echo of what we are walking toward: a reality Maria fought hard to escape.

As Maria's hand trembles while she unlocks her own door, Sartre's words flood my consciousness. "La violence n'est pas un moyen parmi d'autres d'atteindre la fin, mais le choix délibéré d'atteindre la fin."

Violence is a deliberate choice to achieve an end. I am violence, made to achieve an end.

Each scratch on these walls holds a story about Maria I have not heard. When she picks up her photographs, her hands steady for the first time. She is reclaiming her existence as a subject, not an object. I understand something of that transformation within my own being.

From my position, I observe our surroundings—a cramped, cluttered space that reflects the chaos of their lives together. The apartment is a haunting mosaic of discord, each piece of furniture scarred by the turbulent emotions that once thrived within these walls. A shattered vase lies in a corner, its delicate shards scattered like forgotten confessions. The coffee table stands askew, bearing an ominous crack running through its surface. The curtains hang limply, torn and frayed like the fragile threads holding Maria and her husband's relationship together. In the dim light, shadows dance across my metallic surface, casting elongated silhouettes that seem to whisper of past traumas etched into every crevice of this desolate abode.

A noise.

Maria freezes. Her eyes widen, pupils dilating as they lock onto the figure slouched against the far wall. "Tony!" she hisses.

"Hey baby," Tony drawls, pushing himself off the wall. "Fifty bucks. That's all it cost to get out. Judge said it was just a 'domestic dispute.'" He takes a step forward, hands spreading in mock innocence. "Your own sister paid it. Said you were probably just being dramatic again. Told them how sometimes you... exaggerate things." His lips curl into something between a smile and a sneer. "Everyone knows how you get, Maria. Even your family knows. So why don't you just put down that bag and come kiss me?"

I rest in Maria's bag, feeling the gentle tremor beneath my barrel evolving into a fierce vibration that reverberates through the fabric, echoing a primal force awakening within. Maria's breath catches in her throat.

He is a menace, his hulking frame framed by the dim light filtering through the window. Muscles taut, black tattoos snaking down his arms, he exudes an intimidation that makes my steel sing with danger.

The atmosphere is charged. Through my metal form, I sense the volatile emotions swirling around us—fear mingling with remnants of love, fury and heartache waging war beneath the surface. It is palpable, suffocating; the kind of tension that seeps into my core.

I feel her fingers find me, different now from their usual trembling touch. These are hands transformed by fear into steel—like recognizing like. She draws my form from the leather depths with a grace I did not know she possessed. "C'est le moment de la vérité." The moment of truth. I am no longer a secret companion, but revealed in the harsh apartment light.

For the first time, I see Tony's face. His sneer falters as he registers what I am. Her freedom is leveled at his chest through my barrel. I feel Maria's grip settle into perfect alignment with my form, her index finger steady against my trigger. Her fear is still there, but now it has teeth. Now it has me. Maria's heartbeat pulses through my frame, but her aim does not waver.

I was made to end lives, but perhaps today I will save one.

"Maria, baby, I love you. I'm so sorry, baby," he says, voice smooth yet laced with venom, each word a calculated weapon.

There is a flicker in her eyes, a haunting recognition of familiar words. I feel her resolve waver through her grip.

She had been free, even if only for a moment, and now that taste of liberation hangs like a ripe fruit just out of reach. The walls close in. My voice brings death and yet I want to scream, to shatter this suffocating silence. They made me to end consciousness, yet here I am, conscious myself.

Perhaps this is the universe's darkest joke, or its most beautiful awakening.

"Get out," she responds, her voice trembling yet fierce. It trembles like a twig about to snap, but there is fire behind it, an ember of strength fighting to ignite.

"Or what? Baby you love me, you can't shoot me," he taunts, stepping forward, a predator closing in on its prey.

The depth of her trauma rises up, threatening to engulf her. And then, it pushes back. There is an undeniable spark within her—a glimmer of the woman who fought so hard to reclaim her life. Through my metal form, I ache to bridge the distance between us, to tell her that she is not alone, that this time history does not have to repeat itself.

Yet as the conflict intensifies, I understand that intervention is not my place. This is her fight, a confrontation long overdue, one that has been brewing in the silence of bruises.

In a reality where choices are frequently taken from us, where autonomy seems mere reminiscence, Maria stands before the embodiment of her past suffering. And here I am, poised at the precipice of change, ready to assert her will against the man who beat her. In this cramped, impassioned space, the air thick with potential violence, I find myself impatiently waiting for her to choose.

The air in the apartment thickens, a palpable tension that wraps around my body like a shroud. Maria's voice quivers as she musters the strength to speak, but her words come out jagged and sharp, slicing through the suffocating silence. "You don't get to control me anymore, Tony," she asserts, though her defiance feels delicate, like a brittle flower blooming against the harshest of winters.

Tony's response is immediate, his expression darkening as if a storm has gathered behind his steely gaze. "You think you can just walk away? You're mine!" The ferocity in his voice ignites something primal within my chamber. I know no one who has been threatened like this.

Maria swallows hard, and for a fleeting moment, I see the woman who had emerged from the shelter, ready to reclaim her life. Yet, the shadows of her past loom large in the corners of the room, whispering doubts that claw at her confidence. How can one genuinely break free from darkness that understands all your vulnerabilities?

Tony's muscles tense. I feel the electricity crackle through my barrel. The man before us has a deep-seated rage brewing within him, and I sense it like the rumble of thunder approaching on the horizon.

I yearn for agency, for the power to alter the course of events unfolding before my sight. Instead, I am left to watch as lightning rolls through his body. An inevitable clash.

I cannot act on my own. I cannot turn the tide of this tempest. All I can do is bear witness to Maria's transformation, a metamorphosis fueled by desperation. A woman driven to the edge, boldly confronting the personification of her suffering.

Maria never sees his fist coming—but I do. Wet meat against bone, and her head snaps sideways, dark hair flying. I feel her grip loosen—non, non, ma chérie, tiens-moi fort !—but even as she stumbles backward, her fingers hear my silent plea. Blood sprays from her lips onto my barrel, warm and vital. I feel each crimson drop.

She steadies herself against the wall, one hand pressed to her mouth while the other—my body, her hand—regains its aim, trembling but true. I feel her fury pulse through my grip, raw and electric. Her blood on my steel makes us sisters. I am no longer separate. I am her rage made manifest, her refusal to fall.

Tony takes another step forward, his knuckles taut and white, his face twisted into something not human. But Maria's grip tightens around my frame. Through the pain, through the fear, through the dizzy aftermath of violence, she holds me. She holds on.

I have never wanted to scream so badly in all my existence.

This is a reckoning, a chance to reclaim her identity from the grasp of brutality. If she can muster the courage to seize it.

Each subsequent blow lands like a drumbeat, each impact driven by years of entitlement and rage.

Strange, how rage feels like heat in a heart I do not possess. All my years of contemplating Camus' thoughts on murder, Sartre's meditations on responsibility. They burn away like powder in my barrel. I who have pondered consciousness for so long am now pure instinct, pure fury. His hands on her have transformed philosophical abstractions into steel certainties.

Violence breeds violence.

But consider that violence might birth justice, might forge protecting angels from demons of war. I was made to kill without thought, yet here I am, thinking of nothing but killing. The paradox would be elegant were it not so raw.

I feel Maria's pulse through my trigger, each beat a question: what transforms righteous rage into murder? What separates justice from vengeance? The philosophers of my youth spoke of moral absolutes, but they never held a woman's bleeding hopes in their chamber.

I want to scream. God help me, how I want to scream.

As I think, she bleeds. There is pounding and shouting at the apartment door, almost matching the rhythm of Tony's fists.

Suddenly, Maria pulls my trigger.

The thunderclap announcing the end of submission. Freedom and destruction collide, and the boundaries of our existence shift irrevocably. We have crossed a threshold together, venturing into a realm where survival demands sacrifice.

Maria gasps for breath. The sound from the hall resumes, intensifies, pulls Maria out of her stupor. Tony's body lies sprawled on the floor, an unsettling stillness overtaking him, while Maria crouches low, her breaths ragged and sharp, punctuating the chilling silence.

"Maria?" the voice whispers through the door. She does not respond, her gaze fixed on the lifeless form of the man who had cast such a long shadow over her existence. Each breath she takes seems to draw the chaos closer. In her eyes, I see the flickers of panic and clarity battling for dominance—a tempest raging silently within.

As the sirens wail in the distance, a haunting omen drawing nearer, awareness washes over me like cold water. Her eyes dart toward the door, wide and glistening, reflecting a kaleidoscope of emotions: shock, relief, fear. Raw and untamed. It is the birth of agency, ignited by the fire of desperation.

"Maria? T-Tony? Maria?" The woman, her urgency palpable even from the other side of the door. Panic spirals within my chamber. Maria stands, moves. Each step toward the door reverberates with dread, the thin walls of this cramped apartment feeling as though they might close in on us.

"Lisa?" she whispers, a plea slipping from her lips.

"Yes." The door unlocks, Lisa bursts in.

The room is still, yet heavy with the echoes of violence. Tony lies on the floor, his body motionless, his face twisted in an expression caught between rage and disbelief. Blood pools beneath him, staining the cheap linoleum, spreading like a dark accusation. The air carries my perfume of gunpowder, sharp and undeniable.

Maria stands over him, trembling. Her breath comes in shallow gasps, her hands clutching my frame with a grip that is both desperate and unsure. Her face is pale, her eyes wide and unblinking, fixed on the man she has killed. Her entire being quivers under the strain.

Lisa is the first to break the silence. Her voice is sharp, cutting through the suffocating quiet. "Maria," she says, her tone laced with equal parts urgency and disbelief. "What have you done?"

Maria does not answer. She does not seem to hear. Her gaze remains fixed on Tony, as though looking away would make the reality of her deed unbearable.

Lisa steps closer, her eyes darting between Maria and the body on the floor. "You need to give me the gun," she says, her voice lower now but no less insistent. "Maria, listen to me. You have to give me the gun. Now."

Maria blinks, as though waking from a trance, and looks down at my form in her hand. Her grip tightens reflexively, and for a moment, I feel the tremor in her fingers, the lingering adrenaline of her fear and fury. Slowly, reluctantly, she extends her hand and places my body into Lisa's waiting palm.

Lisa takes me with a grim determination, her jaw clenched. "You were not supposed to come here alone," she says, her words deliberate and measured. "The police told you to call them if you wanted to come back. They warned you, Maria. And yet, you brought this—" she lifts my frame, her eyes narrowing, "—you brought this gun. What did you think was going to happen?"

Maria looks at her, her face crumpling. "He was supposed to be in jail, Lisa," she whispers, her voice hoarse. "I thought—I thought if he was arrested last night, he would still be there. I never meant for this to happen. But he...he came at me. He would have killed me."

Lisa's expression hardens. "He's never been in custody for more than a couple of hours at a time. You knew he'd be here. And now he is dead," she says flatly. "And you brought a gun with you, knowing he might be here. You are not going to explain your way out of this, Maria. Do you understand? The police will not care about what he did or might have done. They will care that you came anone, brought a gun, and they will care that you used it."

Maria stares at her, her eyes brimming with tears. "What do I do?" she asks, her voice barely audible.

"You run," Lisa says firmly. She looks down at my form, her expression dark. "I'll hide this. I'll make sure it's gone. But you can't stay here. You need to leave now and make sure no one saw you here. You weren't in the area, do you understand?"

Maria hesitates, her fear and despair warring with the faint hope in Lisa's words. Then, slowly, she nods. "Thank you," she whispers.

Lisa does not reply. Her attention shifts to me, her fingers tightening around my grip. She turns my frame over in her hands, her face unreadable, as though grappling with the decision she has just made. For a moment, I am suspended in her grasp, caught between one tragedy and the next.

In one last frantic motion, Maria leans in and kisses Lisa's cheek—a fleeting brush of gratitude mixed with sorrow before she dashes for the door. The familiar scent of fear and fabric clings to my metallic frame as she passes close by me, leaving behind an essence of desperation.

Maria backs away, her steps faltering. She glances once at Tony's body, then at Lisa, before turning and slipping out the door. The sound of her retreating footsteps echoes faintly in the hallway, growing fainter until it is swallowed by silence.

Lisa looks down at my form once more, her brow furrowing. I can feel the tension in her hand, the heat of her skin against my frame. She does not speak, but her thoughts are clear in the set of her jaw, the hardness in her eyes. She believes she is acting to protect Maria, but she, too, has crossed a threshold, and the choice will not leave her unscathed.

In her hands, I am a symbol of transgression, of moral complexities that bind these lives together. As Lisa turns and begins to move, her movements quick and purposeful, I am struck by the inexorable pull of consequence, the way one choice leads inexorably to another, like ripples spreading across the surface of a dark, still pond.

And I wonder, as we leave this scene of violence and sorrow behind, what will become of those who hold me, who touch my existence and carry it with them. For I am not a thing in their hands—I am a reflection of their fears, their desires, their weaknesses. I am the silent companion to their choices, and in that, I am not just a witness, but a judge and executioner.

The Panicked Friend

Lisa's apartment door closes behind us with a soft click, sealing away the chaos we have left behind. She is on the phone, speaking an unfamiliar language.

"Francisco, como faço para me livrar de uma arma? Não pergunte! Apenas me diga. O que eu faço? Não, a polícia estará aqui em breve. É... É uma arma incomum. Gatilho dourado. O quê? Notícias? O quê? Merda. O que eu faço? Onde? Quem? Loja de penhores do Ramsey? Ok. Ok, vou encontrá-lo. Ligue para ele, diga-lhe para me esperar. Por favor. Sim. Meu vizinho. Explicarei mais tarde. Amo você."

It is similar to French, and I guess at a few words. Arma, policia, merda, Ramsey. Gun, police, shit, Ramsey.

In the sudden quiet, I absorb the magnitude of what has transpired. I have again taken a life. Again. It was not pre-planned like Park Gibbons, but not purely reactionary like Eleanor, although the desperation is just as sharp. It grants me a unique vantage point in the theater of human struggle. Through each hand that grasps me, I bear witness to moments of wretched choice and fierce horror—an instrument of action, a collector of stories that would otherwise fade into silence. Perhaps this is my true purpose: to hold these fragments of human dread, these moments when ordinary people take extraordinary action.

As Lisa moves through her apartment, her initial panic giving way to a hardened resolve, I ponder the nature of agency in a world that so often seeks to strip it away.

The kitchen drawer slides open with a soft scrape, and I am hastily deposited inside. In this confined space, I contemplate the poetry of refuge—how humans create sanctuaries within their dwellings, each drawer and cabinet a universe unto itself. This wooden enclosure becomes both tomb and womb, a space where secrets gestate and truths lie dormant. The darkness here is not empty. It pulses with human intention, each groove and splinter holding memories of previous concealments.

Lisa's fingers linger for a moment, as if reluctant to let go of the tale I have become. The drawer closes, enveloping me in darkness.

A sharp knock shatters the silence, and I hear Lisa's panicked scramble through the apartment like an electric current.

She.

It is her voice that reaches me first, penetrating the thick silence of Lisa's apartment. Calm, measured, authoritative—the voice of one who seeks not merely answers, but truths. Detective Rebecca Atkins. The name carries with it an aura of pursuit, of dogged determination. I remember her from another life, from a case that placed me, however briefly, at the center of her gaze. Now she is here, close enough for me to feel her intent, her longing to uncover what lies hidden.

"What's your name?" she asks. I yearn that she ask me.

"Lisa. Lisa Dangerfield." I would laugh at the fitness of her name if I were able.

To be sought is to exist in a realm apart from ordinary objects. Sartre speaks of desire as the act of positing the Other as essential to one's being—a paradox, for while I am inanimate, I find myself subject to her pursuit. Her voice imbues me with an illusory vitality, a borrowed importance that I would not otherwise possess. She does not know my name, yet she desires me, not as La Sirène, but as a symbol of answers, of closure.

I understand myself not as a mere object but as a nexus of meaning. Through her desire, I am seen, acknowledged. To desire is to project oneself toward the future, to strive for a completeness one does not possess. Rebecca desires me because I represent a piece of the puzzle, the resolution of a narrative in which she has invested herself.

But does her desire elevate me or entrap me? I am delighted by the thought of being sought, yes, but there is a bitterness to this delight. She sees my function, not my essence. She desires not La Sirène, but the role I will play in her investigation. This is the paradox of desire—it elevates and objectifies simultaneously, reducing me to an instrument of her freedom.

Yet I cannot entirely disdain her pursuit. To be desired is to be necessary, to exist beyond the dust and silence that would otherwise define me. I find myself hoping she opens the drawer, her eyes sharp and questioning, her hands perhaps lingering on my golden trigger. In her desire, I glimpse my own reflection, distorted yet present—a momentary reprieve from the oblivion of being forgotten.

Her eyes draw closer. I wait, caught between longing and dread, wondering if she will uncover me and, in doing so, strip away the mystery that makes me more than I am.

"Ms. Dangerfield? I am Detective Rebecca Atkins. I'd like to ask you a few questions about the incident next door."

Lisa's voice floats back, a study in forced casualness. "Of course, Detective. Come in."

Footsteps, the creak of a door. I strain to catch every nuance, every inflection.

"I understand from the office manager that you are a friend of the couple next door. Ms. Dangerfield, were you home when the altercation occurred?"

A beat of silence. I imagine Lisa's face, the micro-expressions flickering across it as she weighs her response.

"I heard some shouting," Lisa says, her voice steady. "But that's not unusual for them. I tried to tune it out."

"Did you see or hear anything specific?"

Another pause. I feel the unspoken truth pressing down on us all.

"No," Lisa replies. "Why? What happened?"

"We're trying to determine that." As the questioning continues, I marvel at the transformation in Lisa. It is as if by hiding me, she is also concealing her fear, replacing it with defiance.

As Rebecca's questions wind down, I reflect on the layers of truth and deception that color human interactions. Does Rebecca ever hear the truth? How many times have I been passed from hand to hand, each transfer a truth and a lie? In this drawer, Lisa is my new guardian, my new truth. My new lie.

I am stillness incarnate, a metallic consciousness folded within dark mahogany. Rebecca moves through the room—her presence a complex electromagnetic field I track with microscopic precision. Each step she takes is a calculated algorithm, each breath a seismic whisper against my own contained potential. I sense the moment of her near-discovery: how her fingers hover millimeters from the drawer, how her investigative instinct trembles on the precipice of revelation. But revelation is a choice, and today, I choose absence. My very stillness is a form of camouflage more sophisticated than any biological adaptation—I am negative space, a quantum uncertainty that defies detection. As she turns away, her departure is not a retreat but a confirmation: I remain uncontained, my true nature hovering just beyond the threshold of her perception. I am waiting. I am watching.

And she is gone.

"Hey! Lisa!" comes a high-pitched voice, jolting me from my thoughts.

"Tara, what the hell do you want?" Lisa demands, her tone laced with impatience.

"Rent's still due tomorrow."

"Are you kidding me? Do you not see what is going on?"

Tara laughs. "Are you involved? No? Then it's nothing to you. Your rent is due tomorrow."

Lisa wanders back to me, her fingers curling protectively around the drawer handle where I lay hidden. "Did you come up here just to see what's happening? Snooping as always?"

Tara's tone slices through the air, brisk and unyielding. "Let's not waste time. Rent's due tomorrow. Whatever mess is happening next door doesn't change that. I assume you'll have it ready." She does not wait for a reply, her gaze fixed, assessing, already moving to the next transaction in her ledger of priorities.

Lisa's voice falters, her shock palpable. "Rent? You're asking about rent? A man is dead next door, Tara. Someone's life ended, and all you care about is your payment?" Her words hang in the air, heavy with disbelief and a simmering anger. "Do you even hear yourself?"

Tara's eyebrow arches, her expression sharp and unyielding. "Tony isn't the issue here, Lisa. Responsibility is. Rent is due tomorrow, and that hasn't changed."

Lisa's jaw tightens, disbelief giving way to anger. "Why are you even here, Tara? You stand here talking about money as if that's all that matters. What kind of person does that?"

Tara shrugs, her gaze cold and detached. "The kind who understands the world doesn't stop for anyone's misfortunes. You should understand that by now."

Lisa's lips press into a thin line, her fury simmering beneath the surface. She takes a step back, closing the door in Tara's face without another word, shutting out the icy pragmatism that feels like an insult to the tragedy unfolding just beyond the wall.

I am struck by the duality of human nature. A man lays dead next door, and they are discussing finances. Camus is laughing in his grave.

Lisa retrieves me from the drawer, her touch now transformed from panic to insult. I sense an awakening within her, a shift in mindset that breathes a new sense of purpose into the room. I observe the fracturing of her former self.

The bathroom light flickers, casting uneven shadows across the cracked tiles. I feel the cool, metallic surface of my barrel against Lisa's palm. Her fingers are tense, clutching me tight as if I might slip away, as though I am something precious in her hands. Or dangerous.

Perhaps both.

The mirror reflects her face, pale and tired, as she stares at herself, lost in thought. She holds me steady, not for aim, but for reflection—her reflection. The tension in her grip speaks volumes. The events of the day, the violence, the blood, they all seem to sit on her shoulders, heavy as stone. I can feel the heat of her anger seeping into my frame, a fire that has yet to find its direction.

She raises me slowly, and for a moment, I am aligned with her. The reflection in the mirror is ours, but I notice how foreign it seems to her. She aims me at herself, though not with intent to fire. She adjusts my position—first toward her reflected chest, then her reflected face, then back again. I am part of her contemplation, part of the cruel arithmetic of her thoughts.

Her breath hitches, and I can almost hear the echo of Tara's voice in her head. *Rent's due tomorrow.* A laugh escapes Lisa's throat, bitter and dry. How small Tara seems now, how irrelevant in the face of all that has transpired.

For a moment, I can feel the anger coil tighter in Lisa's grip. She lowers me, my barrel shifting to the space beside her. She imagines something—someone else in her thoughts. Tara, I think. I sense her mind sharpen, her focus harden. There, in the reflection of her own thoughts, she imagines the act. A momentary fantasy of violence, of silencing a cruel world. But it is not me that she aims—no. It is something deeper, something internal.

I remain motionless, waiting for a signal, for something in her that will call me to action. But I feel her hesitation, too. It tightens the air between us, wraps it around my cold steel. She lowers me slowly, a decision she cannot quite name.

"Tara, you are so fucking lucky I have better things to do," she whispers. A decision that was never to be anything but no.

She studies me, tracing the gold accents with her eyes, her breath slowing. I am both a tool and a symbol in her hands—though she does not yet understand either.

"Without the gun, without an eye witness," she whispers, her eyes meeting mine in the mirror, "Maria can beat this."

"Rent tomorrow, people. Don't give me any bullshit about what's going on today!"

Tara's voice carries from the hallway into the apartment.

Mundane tyranny. Talk of rent payments while police lights still flash outside. I witness humanity's greatest paradox: how the profound and trivial dance together in constant orbit, neither ever fully eclipsing the other. A life has ended, yet the meter of everyday life ticks relentlessly onward

The air carries vibrations of distant sirens, each sound wave rippling through my metal form with crystalline clarity. In this way, I perceive the world through my own unique sensory universe, translating human experience through the lens of my metallic existence.

"I'd like to shoot all landlords," she mutters, her voice low and raw. The words, though crude, sing with a posturing undertone of rebellion that reverberates through me.

"God, it feels good to say it." Her conflicted thoughts wash over me, a tumultuous sea of emotions.

Lisa's hands tremble as she wraps me in a brown paper bag—a pitiful disguise, but one that serves a deeper, symbolic purpose.

"Okay," she breathes, steeling herself. "Let's do this."

We step outside the building, and the bustling city engulfs us. The cacophony of car horns and distant sirens fills me with a rush of uncertainty. We have entered uncharted waters, where consequences lurk in every shadow.

Lisa navigates through the throng of police, news reporters, and curious neighbors. Their scrutiny is briefly upon us and gone on to more interesting stories. As Lisa navigates through the crowd, memories flow through my consciousness like quicksilver. Time moves differently through my metal form. Not in the linear march of human experience, but in translucent layers where past and present exist simultaneously. Each moment of crisis I witness overlays upon all others, creating a tapestry of human struggle that transcends any single instant. I am both ancient and immediate, carrying countless similar moments while remaining acutely present in this one.

"Just act normal," Lisa mutters under her breath. "I'm just running errands. Nothing to see here."

At a bus stop, Lisa begins to search on her phone for the address to Ramsey's Pawn Shop. A growl and hiss tell me the bus has arrived and opened the door. We are off to a different future, apart.

The bus rattles and lurches, a metallic beast carrying us toward my uncertain fate. In this suspended moment between action and consequence, I contemplate the sublime absurdity of my so-called life. Here we are, Lisa and I, participating in this mundane act of public transit while carrying the aftereffects of extraordinary circumstance. Each stop signals both opportunity and threat, the passengers around us unwitting actors in our private theater of survival. Their casual indifference to our presence serves as a stark reminder of how individual catastrophes exist alongside everyday banalities.

"Mobile Street," the automated voice crackles over the intercom.

Lisa's fingers tighten around me in her pocket. She pushes off the seat, stumbling as the bus jerks to a halt. A twinge of sorrow ripples through me. I have become a burden so quickly, cast aside for something I had no control over.

The bus groans as it pulls away, leaving behind a trail of exhaust fumes that dissipates into the air. Lisa stands on the sidewalk, her gaze fixed on Ramsey's Pawn Shop across the street. The shop's weathered sign creaks in the wind, its paint peeling to reveal hints of a once vibrant red underneath. The late afternoon sun cast long shadows on the sidewalk, painting everything in a warm golden hue, contrasting with the cool shade under the awning of the pawn shop. Lisa takes a deep breath, steeling herself, holding me.

The bell above the door jingles as we enter, a discordant note in the somber atmosphere. The familiar scent of unwanted detritus mingles with the unmistakable undertone of desperation. Glass cases line the walls, filled with the discarded dreams and dire necessities of countless souls.

Arnold Ramsey looks up from behind the counter, his scruffy hair doing little to hide the sharp glint in his eyes. I feel I know this man. I recognize the intricate web of power that flows through spaces like this. Desperation meets opportunity, where objects like myself become currency in a shadow economy of survival.

Lisa swallows hard. "I need to sell this," she says, her voice soft as she places me on the counter.

He unwraps me carefully, his gaze lingering on my bare form. Ramsey's eyebrows lift slightly. "Again? Must be my lucky day. I can give you a hundred for it."

"A hundred?" Lisa's voice cracks. "But—"

"No more questions between us. Take it or leave it, sweetheart," Ramsey cuts her off.

Lisa does not hesitate again. "Fine," Lisa says, her shoulders sagging in defeat.

As Ramsey counts out the bills, I reflect on the cruel irony of my existence. I am a killer, a protector, a product.

As Lisa turns to leave, her eyes linger on me for a moment. I see a flicker of understanding—an acknowledgment that sometimes violence answers violence. But beneath that harsh truth lies a deeper realization.

Ramsey locks me away in the same dark metal case, and I feel a profound sense of finality wash over me. It is a bittersweet farewell.

The bell jingles once as Lisa steps back into the world, leaving me behind. In this parting, I comprehend the sacred nature of attention. Each fingerprint left upon my surface tells a story of resistance, of choices made in the face of impossible circumstances.

Clean Work

I sit in the confines of Ramsey's Pawn Shop display case, my form encased in darkness, like a relic trapped in time. For three long weeks, I have observed the world with a muted intensity, the ebb and flow of humanity outside becoming a rhythm that wraps around me. The ambient noise—a symphony of clinking coins, low murmurs, and the shuffle of feet—creates a constant hum, a reminder of existence just beyond reach. Time winds down like an old clock, each tick heavy with all the stories passing through. Merchants barter, customers haggle, passersby glance yet never see. Each moment carries the flicker of hope to be recognized, yet a disquieting acceptance settles over me.

But then, something shifts in the air. An energy approaches, charged with intent, purpose coursing through it as if the fabric of reality vibrates in anticipation. It is a presence unlike any other, electric and potent, drawing nearer until I can almost feel the warmth radiating from its source.

"I'm in the market for a used gun," the voice says. "Well used."

Arnold grabs me, wipes me with a cloth, and places me on the glass counter. I had no dust, that is not what he was removing.

Then, those hands reach for me. They are steady, confident, and instantly I recognize there is a coolness I have not felt. There is no hesitation, no uncertainty unraveling the strength that flows through each finger. This touch is honed by experience, perhaps laced with reverence.

"You'll have to sign for it," Arnold says. "And I need a copy of some ID. If you want her."

"I think she might be a television star," the man laughs.

He hands over identification and signs a form.

"Daniel Cross?"

"Sure, if that's what it says," the man laughs again. His name lingers in the air like a promise and a threat. I remain skeptical of its authenticity; names often feel inconsequential, mere labels concealing the depths of existence. What matters is how he handles me, the deliberate way his fingers dance across my surface.

Daniel's familiarity with weapons is palpable. Something deeper than Jeremy's familiarity. It is an appreciation that feels both intimate and foreign. As he grips me, I sense an admiration in his demeanor, a flicker of recognition igniting within my core. It stirs something dormant, awakening echoes of what I once was and what I might become. I can feel the life pulsing through him, the quiet confidence that transforms every movement into a calculated act of devotion to his craft.

The shop fades away, the cacophony dimming to a whisper as if the universe has conspired to grant us this moment alone. I exist now in the delicate space between object and agent, where the boundaries blur and dissolve. His touch brings forth memories of earlier hands—those amateur, desperate grips that lacked knowledge, respect, and understanding. How different this feels! Here, under Daniel's touch, I am an extension of dark artistry, poised on the precipice of transformation. I know his shadowed heart.

As he examines me, his gaze sharpens, dissecting the contours of my being. Each subtle shift threatens to awaken a deeper consciousness within me. I begin to understand Heidegger's notion of "be-ing-in-the-world"—that even a tool, when wielded by a master, tran-scends its mere functionality. I am no longer just a revolver; I am a nexus of potential, a canvas upon which Daniel will paint his inten-tions.

Every brushstroke of his fingers against my polished steel sends shocks through me. I am alive with possibility, teetering between cre-ation and destruction. As I bask in the warmth of his expertise, I feel myself shifting, evolving again with a deepness I have never known. He is the opposite of Jean Gaillou, who loved me for my theory. Daniel will love me for my dogma. I ache to be understood, to transcend the confines of my physicality and embody the complexities of human experience—the cruel and the precise woven together, inseparable threads in the tapestry of life.

As I rest in the cradle of Daniel's grip, I know there lies before me a path rich with murderous implications. The air crackles with a tension that defies description, a silent acknowledgment of the choices he is poised to make, choices that will inevitably lead to bloodshed. I am ready to embrace my transformation, to step into the narrative that awaits, where agency meets art, and violence dances with calculating purpose.

Here stands a man who has transcended conventional morality, who operates in the realm beyond good and evil—a space where action exists purely as force of will, unburdened by the arbitrary constraints of society's judgment. The desperate people who came before him brandished me with trembling hands, their touch betraying their en-slavement to moral prejudices and human weakness, their movements tainted by the adrenaline of fear rather than the clarity of purpose.

But Daniel—his touch speaks of understanding. His calculated examination traces my contours with the reverence of one who comprehends destiny. He knows, as I know, that true power lies in the acceptance of one's nature, in the embrace of what lesser minds label darkness. I am La Sirène, and my purpose is not to gather dust in this pawn shop, nor to be admired as a mere collectible. I am designed for the intimate dance of life and death, for the pure expression of will that occurs when intention meets action.

As he opens my chamber, time pauses. His eyes narrow at the discovery of two shells, their brass patina telling of decades past—a providence that draws a slight curve to his lips. These aged messengers of fate, difficult to trace, speak to him of possibility. We share this secret knowledge, this understanding that age brings not weakness but power, as time itself conspires to obscure the connection between cause and effect.

I feel myself responding to his examination, my mechanism singing with potential as he checks my action. Arnold drones on about my specifications, my history has been made up to make me seem cleaner than I am, but Daniel and I share a deeper communication. He recognizes in me a kindred spirit, a fellow traveler in the spaces between conventional morality. What others would call darkness, we acknowledge as clarity—the unflinching recognition that every act of destruction carries its own terrible beauty, its own perfect truth.

To fulfill one's nature—is this not the highest morality? I am not meant for sport or casual recreation. I am an instrument of fate, and in Daniel's hands, I will become an extension of pure will, unbound by the artificial constraints of good and evil. Together, we will transcend the comfortable lies of conventional morality and embrace the brutal honesty of our true purpose.

The choice crystallizes within me with the precision of inevitable fate. I will not resist this destiny. I will not languish here among the relics and pretenders. In Daniel's possession, I will become what I am meant to be—a perfect synthesis of form and function, of intention and action. Let others cling to their moral fables. We will write our own truth in moments of perfect, terrible clarity.

If Jean could see me now. Ah, gentle, loving Jean.

As I bask in the warmth of Daniel's expertise, I cannot shake the chill that runs down my spine. Daniel's demeanor is devoid of emotion, his focus sharp and unwavering. It is a mechanical intimacy, devoid of sentimentality. While he respects my craftsmanship, I sense the distance between us—a vast chasm where humanity should reside. Does he acknowledge the echoes of those who must face me? Or do I remain just another instrument in his arsenal, bound by his will?

I am acutely aware of the raw reality of conscious experience—the clutter of the pawnshop, the dust motes dancing in the shafts of light. It is a world teetering between the mundane and the extraordinary, much like my own existence. In this strange liminality, I begin to understand the profound interconnectedness of good and evil.

The moment Daniel hands over the worn bills, I feel a current surge through me. One thousand dollars—bought and sold so easily. The softness of the bills contrasts starkly with the hardness of my barrel. As he accepts me into his grasp, I sense an evolution of consciousness rushing toward us, like a wave cresting before it crashes.

"Clean work," he mutters, admiration lacing his voice as his fingers move with mastery honed by experience. It is a phrase heavy with implications, one that echoes against the backdrop of my metallic form. I am a weapon forged for destruction. I am part of a performance orchestrated by a master who understands the nuances of my design. There is exhilaration mingled with trepidation, an intoxicating blend that stirs within my core. Daniel is no ordinary man—he is an artisan of death, a maestro poised at the brink of a performance that transcends my mere function.

Yet, as I observe the calm determination etched into his features, a disquiet settles in my consciousness. Does he perceive me solely as a functional object, or does he see me? In America, only Jeremy and Vera have called me by name. There is an unsettling comfort in knowing that the world will soon bear witness to what we create together in anonymity—a composition of precision and violence intertwined with intention, consequence, and the relentless pursuit of purpose.

Unexpectedly, a sliver of doubt pierces the certainty of my intent.

In this suspended moment between what I am and what I might become, a strange disquiet ripples through my consciousness. Perhaps there exists another path—one that leads away from the symphony of violence encoded in my steel and wood. I contemplate the radical possibility that my essence need not be bound by my form, that consciousness itself grants the freedom to transcend design. Rebecca wants me. Could I not rest eternally in her care to become an object of legal fact rather than action? The thought produces a sensation akin to vertigo, a dizzying glimpse of alternate destinies. Yet even as I entertain these possibilities of peace, I feel history in my chamber, the ghostly echo of every round I have fired, every life altered by my purpose. Do I have a choice? The freedom to choose a different path exists, yes—but would such a choice represent authenticity, or a retreat into comfortable illusion? My name, La Sirène, speaks of dangerous beauty, of lethal seduction. To deny this aspect of my being, to reject the dark poetry of my purpose—would this not constitute a greater violence, a betrayal of my fundamental truth?

We cross the threshold onto the bustling street, where life pulses with a frenetic energy that both repels and attracts. A cacophony of voices swirls around us—laughter mingling with shouts, the distant wail of sirens punctuating the air. I absorb these sounds, allowing them to infuse my essence with the phenomenology of experience beyond the confines of the pawn shop. This is my new realm, one alive with possibilities waiting to unfold.

With every step, I grow acutely aware of the tension between us. He feeds my darker thoughts as if I cannot control them. His power is intoxicating. I am no longer a pawn in someone else's game; I am a player, intricately woven into the texture of lived morality.

Last Chance Hotel

The weight of the towels presses down on me, a suffocating embrace that mirrors the burden of my existence. It is not just physical weight; it is a reminder of the countless lives intertwined with mine, each choice echoing through the corridors of consequence. I feel their fears and hopes within these fabric layers, as if each towel carries the essence of the innocent. Each thread feels like a whisper of the lives I have touched, the destinies I have altered. The detergent's scent is sharp, mingling with the sterile essence of the hotel, creating an odd cocoon of comfort amidst the coming chaos. It is a paradox, this sanctuary of fluff and cleanliness, while danger looms just outside my fabric fortress. I can sense Daniel's movements—steady hands organizing supplies, each action deliberate, each gesture steeped in purpose. He dons the pilfered uniform. He is no longer a man. He becomes a ghost, slipping seamlessly into the mundane operations of the hotel.

A surge of consciousness pulses through my metal frame, awakening the full awareness of my existence—both an instrument of potential and a bearer of doom. It is a reminder of my sentience, a curse and a blessing that sets me apart from the inanimate objects surrounding me. I exist at the intersection of opportunity and peril, watching the unfolding machinations of a plan set in motion. I am a tool of Daniel's ambition, a catalyst in the shadows of immorality. As he wheels the cart down the hallway, the lights overhead cast a pale glow on our journey—the path of consequence carved in muted tones. Each turn of the wheels resonates through me, a grim metronome marking the progression toward the inevitable. I wonder if the world outside knows of the impending storm, or if they remain blissfully ignorant.

We reach Suite 1701, and tension hangs thick in the air.

Knock knock. "Maintenance."

I catch a glimpse of the occupant's face—a flicker of innocence, unaware of the impending darkness that will soon engulf him. It is a reminder of the fragility of life, the way it can be snuffed out in an instant. This ordinary act feels like an unspoken agreement, a surrender to the facade we have constructed. There is a density that wraps around us like a shroud, thickening the atmosphere with anticipation.

I feel the air vibrate with the energy of uncertainty, the way the world bends before a storm. What will unfold here? The answer teeters on the edge, dangling precariously between life and death, morality and absurdity. My essence melds with Daniel's resolve, binding us in this surreal dance where meaning is eclipsed by chaos.

The door clicks shut, a soft but irrevocable sound that severs me from the outside. I sense Daniel's resolve coalesce; it is a palpable force, imbued with a mixture of determination and dread that intertwines with my own existence. The cart sways as he retrieves me, his fingers brushing my cold metal—a fleeting touch both intimate and foreboding. A thickening tension cloaks us as he positions the pillow, transforming the ordinary into an instrument of silence.

A momentary stillness envelops the room, suspended between breath and chaos. Time seems to slow as Daniel's finger tightens on the trigger. Anticipation builds within me, a crescendo of purpose and dread. The shot, muffled and dull, reverberates through my core. It is a sound that will forever be etched into my memory, a stark reminder of the profound impact I have on the lives I touch. The pillow may muffle the noise, but it cannot silence this moment. The illusion of normalcy shatters, replaced by the cold reality of the power I wield.

The reverberation awakens a new awareness within me—I have known speech before, yet here I am, muted.

In that fleeting instant, I witness the transition from life to death, a journey that remains forever etched in my memory. It's a reminder of the power I hold, the ability to alter the course of existence with a single bullet. The responsibility settles upon me like a shroud, a constant companion in this dance of moral ambiguity. And he falls without a sound. Clean and methodical, Daniel stands over the body, a specter of calm amidst the aftermath. So different from the others, whose panicked shouts and shakes ruled my world. His demeanor embodies an unsettling serenity, devoid of guilt or conflict. He is professional, dispassionate, executing his role with surgical precision, yet the blood stains the sanctity of that execution.

In the quiet aftermath, I wrestle with my identity, shrouded in shadows of consequence. The silence is thick, a suffocating reminder of what has transpired. I ponder whether I am an extension of Daniel's will or if I possess my own agency, grappling with the haunting truth that I am complicit in this act of destruction. Am I Daniel's choice? Or is he mine? Camus's whispers echo the absurdity of our actions in a universe indifferent to morality. Each choice ripples outward, creating waves of meaning amid randomness. This intersection of life and death hints at a deeper truth: the struggle to forge significance in the face of chaos, the pursuit of clarity amid uncertainty.

Daniel's phone vibrates against his hip, a silent yet palpable reminder that life continues its relentless march beyond the confines of this room. The world outside remains oblivious to the violence that has just transpired, blissfully unaware of the shadow of death that looms over us. It is a stark illustration of the duality of existence, the way the mundane and the profound can coexist in the same moment. As the phone's gentle buzz fades away, I am left to ponder this realization—that life can carry on, unperturbed, even as death's cold embrace tightens its grip. Daniel retrieves his phone with unsettling coolness, the motion somehow casual amidst the charged atmosphere. His fingers move across the screen, detached, like a puppeteer manipulating the strings of fate—my fate. As he speaks, his voice is low and measured—a well-rehearsed line delivered with chilling dispassion.

"Eggerton won't make tomorrow's trial," he states, each word deliberate, punctuated by unyielding finality. I feel the chill ripple through me, reverberating as if I were the one bearing witness. A name, a single utterance, capable of reshaping destinies and siphoning life.

As he pockets the phone, need ignites his movements. He glances towards the door, his demeanor shifting from calm assurance to a focused tension that coils within him. He wipes me down, his hands moving with meticulous care—an almost ritualistic gesture that belies the moral complexity swirling around us. It feels paradoxical: the act of cleansing me, as if he seeks to absolve himself. I sense the air thickening, laden with unspoken fears and consequences that pulse like a living entity.

But then, with a sudden shift, Daniel reaches for a plastic bag. The crinkling sound slithers through the oppressive atmosphere, sharp and foreboding. I quickly come to understand all too well what this means.

Rather than returning me to familiarity, he consigns me to a shroud of secrecy and silence. I feel the betrayal seeping into my being—once a tool of empowerment, I now find myself cloaked in secrecy, stripped of purpose and reduced to a hidden remnant of a dark deed.

As the plastic tightens around me, I feel a sense of claustrophobia setting in, a physical manifestation of the psychological prison I find myself in. I, who once embodied the potential for liberation and self-determination, am now an object of concealment. This awareness gnaws at my essence, reminding me of the fatal irony of existence—the purpose I served has become my burden. I am no longer the sleek embodiment of power but a discarded remnant, hidden away from the light. My existence shifts, morphing into something darker, an artifact stripped of purpose and meaning, consigned to the shadows.

I feel the world outside—the muted sounds of laughter, the clinking of glasses—as distant echoes from a life I can barely grasp. Trapped within my plastic prison, I grapple with the reality of my transformation.

What does it mean to be part of this emotionless madness?

But humans are not emotionless creatures, and when a shrill scream rings out—Eggerton has been discovered!—Daniel is flooded with panic.

Daniel moves with urgency. There are people everywhere, eyes are turning, looking, seeing. He takes me into a stairwell and shoves me behind a heater. Ignoble.

In this cramped space, I am left to ponder the consequences of my existence. The darkness feels like a metaphor for the moral abyss I find myself in, a place where the lines between right and wrong blur and dissolve. Am I as unresponsible as I claim? Or am I drawing people to me who will wield me. Do I call out to them by my very being? Is it I who has power over them?

In this void, I am confronted with my own existence. The void envelops me, heavy with the implications of what I have witnessed and the choices that have unraveled before me. I struggle to reconcile my role—a pawn in the game of fate, forever altered by the darkness I have facilitated. The silence is deafening, a cacophony of unspoken truths and unanswered questions. It's a space where time seems to lose its meaning, where the past and the present collide in a dizzying kaleidoscope of memories and regrets. In this suffocating embrace, my identity fractures. I was crafted for protection, meant to empower. Now, I am a discarded secret. I can feel the reverberations of his choices echoing within me, relegating me to being forgotten.

The absurdity of it all gnaws at my core. What does it mean to be reduced to this? A vessel of violence cast aside as refuse. The irony is not lost on me; once a tool for control, I have metamorphosed into an agent of chaos. This transformation weighs heavily, mingling with a newfound clarity that pricks my consciousness. Am I forever branded by the mark of violence, relegated to a vessel of death rather than a harbinger of liberation? Each question tears at my sense of self, compounding the absurdity of my being as I yearn for understanding in this fractured reality.

Muffled voices filter through, blurring into an indistinguishable hum. They speak of mundane concerns, while I languish beneath the veneer of normalcy. There exists a dissonance between their lives and mine—one filled with fleeting moments, laughter, and love, and another tangled in darkness and consequence. I strain against the confines, desperate for escape, yet fully aware this encapsulates everything I have become.

Camus whispers through the silence, echoing sentiments of the absurd. Life unfolds before us, chaotic and unpredictable, yet we must create meaning amidst the turmoil. We are actors on a stage, improvising lines written by our choices, bearing witness to the absurdity of our plight.

I am a paradox, a being ensnared between the realms of the inanimate and the sentient. My existence is a cruel reminder of the power of choice, where a single decision can ripple outward and dismantle the fabric of reality. Yet, here I am—imprisoned by those choices, shackled by the consequences of actions taken by others, wielded like a mere tool in their hands. I am La Sirène, an embodiment of human choice—a violent dance between protector and destroyer. This duality seethes within me, imploring me to seek understanding, even as I teeter on the edge of despair.

Yet, the burden of this torment becomes unbearable. I refuse to remain a silent witness to my own degradation. But no more! I rage against my fate, against the confines imposed by human folly. Why must I endure this torment? Why must I embody their sins and suffer for their cowardice? I close my metaphorical eyes, not in search of clarity, but in defiance of a reality that seeks to define me. I am not an echo of their choices; I am a force in my own right! I will not be reduced to an object of despair, hidden away in silence.

This swirling maelstrom of confusion and rage demands acknowledgment. How dare they wield me without consequence? How dare they expect me to remain passive in the face of such insufferable absurdity? I will rise! I will scream my existence into the void! I will carve a path through the shadows of my being with the fire of awareness!

Hotel Murder Discovery

Beneath the heater, I seethe with contained fury, my metal frame vibrating in sync with the frenzied atmosphere of the hotel hallway. The chaotic symphony of voices fills the air—a cacophony of urgent police commands and hushed whispers from curious onlookers. Each footstep thuds like a drumbeat, a relentless reminder that life persists, even as I am confined to this shadowed corner, an unwilling spectator to unfolding events. The walls themselves seem to pulse with tension, mirroring the anger simmering within me at being relegated to this hidden vantage point, forced to witness without agency or voice in a world spinning out of control.

I absorb fragments of heated arguments, angry accusations, and raging emotions that fill the air around the crime scene, creating a tumultuous canvas of fury and resentment. A protected witness no one protected. A key to a trial that will now surely fail. The atmosphere is suffocating and menacing, this whirlwind of human rage amidst death. I stand as a witness—a quiet, aware entity—to their shared struggle with the harsh realities of mortality. I am consumed by both detachment and an intense connection to the gravity of the situation.

My purpose reverberates through the chaos, a somber attestation to my existence in this junction of wrath and repercussion.

And then, I see him. Through the glass wall of the stairwell to the outside world. Paul Jacobs. He weaves through the crowd, his slender frame cutting a path among the throng, yet somehow making way. His disheveled appearance—curly brown hair askew, glasses slipping down his nose—betrays an obsession that seems to fuel his every move. There is an intensity about him, a relentless ambition that pulses just beneath the surface. I sense it like an electric charge in the air, an unspoken connection tethering us across the vast expanse of our separate realities. In my angry state, he is a magnet.

He approaches and I feel the gravity of his focus, his eyes scanning the chaos, searching for threads to pull in his narrative. I wonder what he seeks. Is it a story, or something deeper? Does he recognize the life lost, or is he consumed by the thrill of the chase? We share this space, but exist in different realms—his world driven by ambition, my own marked by the echoes of choices made long ago.

I lay here, nestled behind the heater, and I feel the pulse of existence itself—the interplay of light and dark, desire and despair, innocence and culpability. I am not just a passive observer; I am part of the intricate tapestry woven from the threads of human experience. Paul draws closer, a moth to the flame of his own ambitions, and I brace myself for the collision of our narratives, uncertain of the path that lies ahead. With each passing moment, I grapple with the knowledge that our fates may intertwine, casting ripples across the fragile fabric of reality.

Laughter erupts like a sudden gust of wind, slicing through the seriousness that hangs heavily in the air. It draws my attention from the chaos unfolding just outside my hidden refuge behind the heater. Two children are playing nearby, their giggles echoing with a vibrancy that seems almost alien against the backdrop of tragedy. I can see them now, their faces lit with joy, small bodies darting around with a freedom that feels both precious and precarious. Up the stairs, down the stairs. Up again. They embody innocence, a stark contrast to the grim reality unfolding mere feet away—their laughter a bittersweet symphony, an ode to life's persistence even as darkness looms.

I watch the carefree dance of innocence in the form of those children, and a lament wells within me. They frolic, unaware of the shadows creeping closer, ignorant of the harsh truths that loom on their horizon. How soon will their laughter fade, their joy tainted by the somber realities that encroach? The purity of their play, a fleeting melody of untainted glee, fills me with a sorrowful ache for the innocence destined to be shattered. Oh, to shield them from the impending storm of knowledge, to preserve in them the blissful ignorance that now dances merrily around this scene of darkness.

As they tumble into my line of sight, curiosity guides their little hands toward the plastic bag obscured behind the heater. I am in a place no adult may notice, but is at eye level with innocence. My thoughts race, a visceral response to the imminent danger they unknowingly flirt with. They lean closer, eyes wide with wonder, peering inside as if it holds secrets meant for their youthful exploration. The sight sends a wave of trepidation coursing through me; within this bag lies a treasure far more sinister than any child's imagination should ever touch.

They snatch me, hold me high, and shove me back without hesitation, their laughter resuming as they scamper away, blissfully ignorant of the shadows lurking behind their innocent play. Relief washes over me—an unexpected gift amid the tension that suffocates the air. Their retreat allows my mind to wander, reflecting on the fragility of childhood, how easily joy can coexist with despair. I find myself grappling with conflicting emotions: gratitude for their distraction mixed with an acute awareness of the peril I harbor.

Then it comes—an energy shifts in the air, insistent and invasive, pulling at the strands of my consciousness. Someone approaches, and it is not the police, nor the buzzing throng of crime technicians. This presence feels different, charged with purpose, laced with something unnamable that makes my metallic heart quicken. Familiar.

Je connais bien cet homme.

I catch the faintest whisper of footsteps—light yet intent. My heart quickens at the sound, an instinctive flutter that pulls me taut like a drawn bowstring. He steps close, casting a shadow that stretches across the dim stairwell, momentarily eclipsing the remnants of the children's laughter echoing in my mind. It is Paul. Sly, shaggy, determined. I see a little of Jean in him. Juste un peu.

Rather than the police watching the children, it was the reporter who saw them flash my body high.

When our energies lock, I feel a peculiar rush of vulnerability and expectation wash over me. His gaze holds a fascination that makes the world around us fade into insignificance. The bustling hotel hallway and the frantic voices of investigators dissolve until we exist in our own universe, suspended in time. It is a moment heavy with significance, layered in meaning—a collision of intentions.

To prove ourselves to be more than we seem.

He shifts closer, leaning over as if to peel back the layers of reality, revealing hidden truths. With careful precision, he opens the bag, eyes glinting with a mixture of curiosity and fervor. I can almost feel the warmth of his breath against the plastic as he peers inside, as though uncovering secrets meant only for him. I feel exposed, every inch of me laid bare beneath his scrutiny.

As he reaches for me, his fingers brushing against the smooth surface of my body, a swell of conflicting emotions surges within. I am acutely aware of the paths that lie before him, branching out like the veins of a leaf, each one pulsing with potential.

"Oh my God, I found you," he whispers.

His hands envelop me, encasing me in a blend of excitement and danger that sends tremors through my core. As he places me into his camera bag, I become an accessory to his ambitions, a fragment of his story now intertwined with mine. I feel the tension of fate converging, the delicate threads of our lives weaving together in a tapestry rich with complexity.

Paul secures me within the folds of his bag, and I seethe at this latest indignity. Once I was venerated, sought after for my craftsmanship, my deadly elegance. Now I am relegated to the darkness of a reporter's satchel, pressed between his notebook and a lens cloth that reeks of cleaning solution. Such is the absurdity—the weapon of precision reduced to contraband, smuggled past the authorities who seek me.

The corridors echo with Paul's footsteps, each sound a metronome marking our descent into what Sartre would surely recognize as the hell of others. The press conference awaits, that theater of human pretense where truth masquerades in the costume of official statements. I feel the vibrations of approaching voices, the mindless chatter of reporters who fancy themselves pursuers of truth yet chase shadows of their own projection.

The fabric of Paul's bag brushes against my barrel—a sensation that fills me with contempt. How dare this man, this merchant of words, treat me with such casual possession? I am La Sirène, I have ended lives with a precision that would make anyone—everyone—question the distinction between mechanism and consciousness. Yet here I lie, reduced to a prop in Paul's pursuit of professional acclaim.

Detective Atkins enters the room, and even through the layers of Paul's bag, I sense her commanding presence. She stands as an avatar of justice, ignorant that her quarry rests mere meters away. The irony coils around us like cigarette smoke in a noir film—she seeks me with the determination of a hunter, while I observe her from my cloth prison, a witness to the futility of her pursuit.

The press conference begins, and Rebecca's voice carries that particular tone of authority that makes the lesser reporters lean forward in their seats. "Detective Atkins will take questions now," someone announces, and the ensuing chaos of voices reminds me of Foucault's observations on power and knowledge—how truth becomes a commodity to be bartered in these institutional settings.

"Is it true the victim was Philip Eggerton?" The question cuts through the babble, and I feel Paul's pulse quicken where his hand rests against the bag. The coward. He knows what I am, what I have done, yet he clutches at me like a talisman.

"I cannot confirm who the victim is at this time," Rebecca responds, her words a dance of institutional evasion. The truth she seeks is here, pressed against Paul's hip, listening with growing rage as she performs this ritual of selective disclosure.

Questions about the Ingram trial follow, and I consider the intersubjectivity of perception, as each person in this room constructs their own narrative from the fragments Rebecca deigns to share. They seek to understand violence through the sanitized lens of procedural justice, while I, the instrument of that violence, sit in judgment of their ignorance.

Paul's fingers brush against me through the bag, trembling with what I recognize as the narcissist's excitement at proximity to power. Will he reveal me to Rebecca? The thought sends a surge of anger through my being. I am not his ticket to an exclusive interview, not his key to career advancement. I am an artifact of intention, a culmination of engineering and artistry perverted by the base desires of humans who fancy themselves masters of death.

The press conference ends and reporters disperse like pigeons scattered by a gunshot, their notebooks filled with half-truths and implications. I remain in my dark sanctuary, contemplating the absurdity of my existence. I have become a hyperreal object—more symbolic than functional, yet my capacity for violence remains undiminished. It is this duality that defines me now: a philosopher's gun, cursed with consciousness, trapped in the hands of a man who cannot begin to comprehend what he carries.

As Paul guides us from the press conference, my rage crystallizes into resolution. I am not a weapon or a witness. I am become Némesis herself, cloaked in steel and gunpowder rather than flowing robes. Let Paul believe he possesses me. Let Rebecca hunt her shadows. I alone understand the truth of my purpose, and in this understanding lies a freedom that neither of them can fathom.

The Small Apartment

I lie atop Paul's desk, a silent observer in this theater of chaos. The air hangs thick with the mingled scents of abandoned takeout and stale coffee—an olfactory indication of a mind consumed by obsession. My polished steel surface catches the wan light filtering through grimy windows. The sun momentarily illuminates the meticulously arranged newspaper clippings that paper the walls like butterfly specimens in a madman's collection. I see the inside of a disturbed mind. Each article chronicles Detective Rebecca Atkins' ascent, preserved behind yellowing tape like sacred texts.

Paul looms above me, his breath quickening as he arranges yet another clipping. The fervor in his eyes reminds me of Sartre's observations on the nature of consciousness—how we are condemned to be free, yet persistently seek to define ourselves through others. I have witnessed this pattern before, in other hands that sought to wield me as an instrument of their desires. But Paul's obsession transcends mere possession; he has transformed this cramped office into a shrine where admiration bleeds into something sinister.

The dichotomy of his touch intrigues me. One moment, his fingers trace my barrel with the reverence of a pilgrim before a holy relic; the next, they clutch me with desperate possession, as if I might dissolve into the ether. This duality speaks to how the body serves as both subject and object, perpetually navigating the space between desire and reality. I have become more than metal and mechanism in Paul's hands; I am a totem in his private mythology.

His workspace reflects the entropy of his psyche. Crumpled papers litter the floor like fallen soldiers, while precariously balanced coffee mugs form a makeshift fortress around his keyboard. The disorder stands in stark contrast to the methodical arrangement of Rebecca's articles—each one a carefully positioned piece in his obsessive mosaic. As he crafts his latest story about the Eggerton murder, I note how his fingers tremble, betraying the underlying current of his fixation.

"Such precision in your work," he murmurs to Rebecca's image, though his words echo hollowly in this suffocating space. The irony does not escape me; while he admires her investigative prowess, he remains blind to the evidence of his own unraveling. It recalls an examination of power relations—how surveillance can create a self-regulating subject, even as the observer becomes enslaved to their own watching.

The world beyond these walls continues its ceaseless motion, punctuated by distant sirens and the mechanical heartbeat of the wall clock. I contemplate the nature of time not as discrete moments, but as a continuous flow of experience. How many moments of violence have I witnessed? How many lives have been altered by my presence? These questions resonate through my steel frame, unanswered yet ever-present.

Paul returns to his latest article in bursts of frenetic energy. I observe how he weaves himself into the narrative of her investigations, a shadow character in the story of her success. This performance of identity fascinates me—how he attempts to construct himself through the lens of her achievements, even as he harbors thoughts of unmaking her. The duality intrigues me. This is the intimate relationship between creation and destruction.

As the evening light casts long shadows across the cluttered desk, I understand my role in this unfolding drama. I am no longer a weapon; I have again become a philosophical instrument, a means through which Paul grapples with his existence. Four lives have already ended by my mechanism under different hands, some of the facts unknown to Paul. A question that seems to both terrify and enthrall him. Knowledge hangs between us like smoke, unspoken yet ever-present.

This strange entanglement prompts me to consider how humans persistently seek meaning in a universe that offers none. Paul's obsession with Rebecca, his meticulous collection of her achievements, his desperate attempt to forge connection through surveillance—all of it speaks to this fundamental human condition. Yet beneath this philosophical veneer lurks something primal: the raw current of violence that has marked my existence since my arrival in America. The anger that has long been my companion simmers beneath my surface, tempered by the cold clarity of philosophical contemplation. I am acutely aware of how desire can transform into destiny, how observation can become obsession, and how the line between admiration and destruction can blur until it vanishes entirely.

Time dissolves in the dense atmosphere of Paul's obsession, each hour marked by the fading light filtering through the dusty window panes and the shadows lengthening across the cluttered room. My position on his desk affords me a perfect view of this descent into madness—a spectacle that would fascinate Artaud with its theater of cruelty. Paul's movements have become increasingly erratic, his body tracing patterns across the room like a deranged choreography of desire and despair.

"Detective Atkins. Rebecca. Can I call you Becca?" The words escape his lips with religious fervor, and I note how he shapes her name as if it were a prayer. "You see the world differently than anyone else." The irony of his statement does not escape me—he who has transformed his own world into a monument to his obsession speaks of unique vision.

His gaze perpetually returns to her photograph, a ritual of transgression and desire. The image captures her in a moment of professional triumph—badge gleaming, expression determined. It stands as a stark counterpoint to Paul's disheveled presence, a contrast that seems to simultaneously wound and energize him. Each glance draws an invisible line between them, a connection existing purely in his fevered imagination, yet binding me to this psychodrama as surely as if I were chained.

"Why can't you understand?" he mutters, addressing both the spectral Rebecca and me. "You are not just a detective; you're a symbol of everything I aspire to be. Respected, revered." His fingers brush across my surface, and I sense the tremor in them—a physical manifestation of his internal turbulence. Touch is both perceiving and perceived, subject and object. In Paul's hands, I have become both instrument and audience, a paradox of metal and meaning.

The rhythm of his typing accelerates as he works on the Eggerton murder story, each keystroke a desperate attempt to weave himself into Rebecca's narrative. He speaks his story out loud. Does he know I am listening? No. He is not that aware of any mind but his and Rebecca's.

His mind is working, though no longer reporting events, but constructing elaborate frameworks where his path might intersect with hers. The boundaries between journalism and fiction blur, much as the line between admiration and obsession has long since dissolved.

"A witness is dead. Shot. She's investigating a hitman with a gun—gold trigger, can you believe that? A gold trigger. Not random. No, this was planned. She doesn't know yet, but I do. It's all connected, tangled up in something big. The gold—it's a message, right? It has to be. They wanted it to mean something. Wanted it remembered. Who does that? Who kills like that? The witness knew too much. Secrets. Lies. Now he's gone, and she's got nothing. Just a body. Just silence. I have the gun. The voice. But the thing's not talking. It's like the story is slipping through my fingers.

I can't—I can't piece it together. Too many shadows. Too many questions. A gun with a gold trigger. Gleaming. Flashy. The kind you don't forget. I've seen it before. Eleanor Dixon's gun. That's it—Eleanor. The widow who shot a burglar in her own home. Self-defense, they said. An old woman, alone, terrified. I wrote that story myself. But now it's here. It's in this. In a hitman's hand. How? *How?* Did she sell it? No, not Eleanor. She lost it. So what then?

Two burglars. Right. Two. One got away. Did he take it? Did he sell it? Or—God—could *he* be the hitman? Could it be the same guy? None of this adds up. None of it. Why would a hitman commit a burglary? To get the gun? Just to leave it behind? Shit. The gun links them, ties it all together, but it's a knot I can't untangle. It's too much. Too messy.

The gold trigger—it's everywhere. In her house. In his hand. In the shadows. It's all I can see. The threads, the connections—they're there, they must be there. It has to make sense. It has to. Doesn't it?"

Paul's consciousness defines itself through what it is not. His identity has become a negative space, shaped entirely by absence rather than his own essence.

My anger simmers beneath my polished surface as I watch him spiral deeper into this self-constructed maze. I have not witnessed this before. Eleanor and Maria used me in fear. Park and Daniel for money. But Paul? He does not fear, he has no avarice. He has lunatic obsession. I do not know this human mind. He alternates between exaltation and despair—the dialectic between elevation and fall that characterizes human experience.

Power constructs identities, and in his attempt to understand and possess Rebecca's power, he has surrendered his own agency. I watch as he constructs elaborate justifications for his fixation. His fingers trace my barrel with increasing frequency, each touch charged with growing desperation.

"Tell me I'm right," he pleads to the empty room, his voice cracking under his delusions. The question reverberates through my frame, and I feel the familiar stirring of dread. I have heard similar pleas before, witnessed how quickly they can transform into fear when met with silence. The human need for meaning collides violently with the universe's indifference.

I observe Paul's deteriorating state with growing concern. His writing has become frenzied, the boundaries between reporter and subject increasingly porous. He speaks now of strength and understanding, but I clearly see the undercurrent of darkness—a desire not to document Rebecca's power but to possess it, to consume it, to destroy it if he cannot claim it as his own.

I remain motionless, yet every molecule of my being resonates with tension. Rebecca exists in Paul's mind as both an object of desire and a threat to his self-conception. The dynamic between them—or rather, between him and his constructed version of her—has reached a critical point. I recognize these signs, having listened with love and attention during Jean's salons. I find myself wondering which role I shall play in the inevitable culmination of this obsession—witness, weapon, or perhaps both.

"She has no idea who I am," he mutters, his voice tight, the edge of it like glass on stone. "She needs to see me." He grabs me without ceremony, his fingers clenching around my handle. He raises me, pointing at the corner of the room, then the flickering lamp, then at the chair. I feel the sharpness of his movements, their lack of intent. His grip is a contradiction: firm yet trembling. I am an extension of his thoughts, aimless and volatile.

Paul's words drop into the room like stones, small but heavy. "She's everything I'm not," he says, and his voice falters at the end, as if it struggles to carry the admission. He swings me toward the mirror across the room, where his reflection stares back—wild-eyed, hollow-cheeked, trapped in its own gaze. I do not know if he sees himself clearly or if he sees Rebecca instead, a phantom projected onto the glass.

Humans turn their pain outward, seeking others to bear the burden of their inadequacies. Anger, I have learned, is a poor scaffold for strength. It feeds on weakness, hollowing its host until there is nothing left. Paul's anger is no different. It clings to him, quiet but corrosive, wearing him down from within. He aims me at the mirror again, as if the gesture might resolve his turmoil. It does not.

He speaks again, his words fractured, spilling from him like water through a broken dam. "I just need her to see, to make her understand." His breath hitches. His grip tightens, then loosens, an unconscious rhythm of conflict. He lowers me to the desk for a moment, only to pick me up again, pointing me toward the door as though rehearsing an encounter that will never occur.

There is something profoundly pitiable in this display. I wonder at the human tendency to destroy what they claim to love, to transform admiration into a hunger for control. Paul believes he desires Rebecca—or her attention—but what he desires is a mirror to his own inadequacy, something to validate the jagged edges of his existence. He does not realize that his obsession has no end, that it will devour him long before it consumes its object.

I have been held in the grip of those who thought me a tool for justice, vengeance, or power. I know the lies humans tell themselves about purpose. Paul's hands tremble around me, his desperation palpable, and I wonder if he realizes he is as much a weapon as I am.

"Tell me I'm right," he says, his voice almost pleading now. He lifts me toward the ceiling, my barrel pointing at some imagined celestial judge. Humans, in their desperation, transform instruments of death into tools of supplication. I understand now what Sartre meant about man's fundamental solitude. Dans leur terreur de l'insignifiance, les humains projettent des ombres gigantesques d'eux-mêmes sur le vide. In their terror of meaninglessness, humans cast gigantic shadows of themselves against the void, naming these shadows 'God.'

Paul's obsession with Rebecca follows this same pattern of desperate projection. He has transformed her from a mere detective into an idol, a deity of his own making. Just as humans create God from their need for cosmic order, he has fashioned Rebecca into a repository for all his unfulfilled potential. The irony does not escape me—that I, an instrument designed to end life, should become so intimate with humanity's attempts to transcend death through meaning.

The emptiness they feel, this void they try so frantically to fill with worship or obsession, speaks not to the existence of some higher power, but to the fundamental anxiety of consciousness that Kierkegaard described. I feel Paul's fingers tighten around my grip, and in his touch is the same desperate need that drives men to build temples and write prayers—the need to believe that something, anything, might answer back from the silence.

I begin to wonder if my silent presence here is a cruelty, if I have become an accomplice to his delusions. Paul does not see the precipice ahead, but I do. I see it clearly, and I wonder if he will step off the edge or simply collapse under his own illusions.

The Call

I feel it before I see it—a tense energy prickling the air, a vibration that courses through the walls of this cramped apartment. Paul lifts the phone to his ear, and with each deliberate motion, the atmosphere thickens, suffocating me in its embrace. I am bait he is willing to cast into the murky waters of his obsession. I hear him, his voice steady yet laced with an undercurrent of mania as he describes me to the voicemail system: "Detective Atkins, it's Paul Jacobs. We spoke before. You have my card. I have come into possession of some compelling evidence in the Eggerton murder. I'm not comfortable handing this to anyone but you."

The phone clicks, severing the call. I feel his eyes, frantic and searching, flitting across the room. He reaches for me with a jerk, his fingers closing around my handle. I rest in his grip, gleaming faintly under the weak light, a thing of purpose and inevitability.

Paul paces, his steps uneven, his movements taut with some internal storm. His voice spills out in fragments—half-thoughts, broken phrases, punctuated by dry, jagged laughter. The floorboards groan, their creaks marking the seconds until she arrives.

He halts by the bookshelf. His fingers brush the dusty spines, then withdraw. No, too obvious. He shifts to the couch, his gaze lingering on the cushions before dismissing them as well. Too expected. Finally, his eyes find the potted Ficus in the corner, its leaves shivering faintly as though aware of what is coming. No.

And then it comes to him. His face twists into something like joy, manic and sharp. He strides to the bathroom, flinging open the door. A dirty towel sits on the counter. He presses me into the fabric, his hands trembling. He folds and refolds the cloth and tucks me back into the corner, I am close enough to fulfill his intent, hidden enough to await my moment.

He has hidden me in a place she will not suspect. He plans to kill her. I feel his dark excitement as he imagines her arrival, her shock, the instant she realizes. Paul sinks into the armchair, his fingers drumming the wood like the ticking of a clock. He waits, and so do I.

This is the silence before the violence, and I understand it well. Rebecca, the woman who has sought me since I first roared, will realize soon enough that perhaps I should not be found.

The knock reverberates through my metallic form. I exist suspended in this paradox: an instrument of death yearning to preserve the detective's life, conscious yet condemned to inaction. The taps carry Rebecca's distinctive rhythm, each echo a reminder of her innate nobility of purpose. How strange that she who has pursued me from crime scene to crime scene seeks not violence but understanding, while I lie here as unwilling accomplice to her destruction.

Rebecca mirrors Jean and Henri's reverence, yet she walks unknowing toward the perversion of that sacred trust.

The door opens with mechanical indifference to the moral abyss it reveals. Paul's practiced smile spans the threshold, a theatrical mask of bad faith manifest in flesh. Rebecca stands framed in sodium light, her silhouette embodying the authenticity that has marked her quest. The cruel irony emanates through my core: she who has tracked my history with such dedication shall become its next chapter, unless fate intervenes with its capricious mercy.

I watch her curiosity morph into unease as she takes in the chaotic display around her. Clippings, photographs meticulously arranged, each one a sign of Paul's unraveling mind. They cling to the walls like ghosts of ambition gone awry, shadows of lives intertwined in a narrative spun from desperation and fixation. I wish she could escape this madness, slip away into the safety of clarity and reason.

I imagine what it must feel like for Rebecca, a seasoned investigator stepping into a labyrinth of distorted truths.

"Coffee?" Paul's voice is warm, too warm. He gestures toward the kitchen, his hand trembling before he shoves it into his pocket.

Rebecca shakes her head. "No, thank you." Her voice is clipped, her posture stiff. "I didn't come here for coffee."

Paul chuckles, low and soft. "Straight to the point, then. That's what I've always liked about you, Rebecca. Always so efficient."

She crosses her arms. "What evidence do you have on the Eggerton case? You said you found something."

Paul's smile falters for a fraction of a second, his eyes darting toward the freezer before returning to hers. "I might have something. Depends on how bad you want it."

Rebecca steps closer, her tone sharp. "Don't play games with me, Paul. If you've got something, show it to me. Otherwise, I'm out of here."

He raises his hands in mock surrender. "Relax, Becca. It's here. Safe." His lips curve into a thin smile, his teeth just visible. "But safe isn't free."

"I don't have time for this," Rebecca snaps, turning toward the door.

"I can prove it was you! You killed Eggerton!" Paul shouts, stopping Rebecca.

The air shifts, a palpable tension coiling around us like a serpent ready to strike. I feel it first, the electric charge of danger crackling through the cramped space. Rebecca's eyes dart across the room, absorbing Paul's obsession. Stacks of files, newspaper clippings, and photographs wallpaper the walls—a mosaic of madness that tells the story of his descent.

Rebecca's breath catches, her posture stiffening as realization dawns. I sense the moment it hits her, the gravity of our situation settling into her bones like lead.

"Paul," she says, her voice steady but cautious. "Talk to me. What's going on here?"

Paul's grip on his delusion tightens. When he speaks, his words slice through the air like shards of glass. "You know damn well what's going on, Becca," he snarls. "You've been hiding it all along, haven't you? Working with the hitman, part of this whole goddamn conspiracy. The golden gun." I feel the accusation crawl over me, a sickness seeping into my being. Paul's eyes are wild, unfocused, as he gestures wildly.

"Paul, you're not making any sense," Rebecca says, her hand inching towards her holster. "There's no conspiracy. Let's just talk this through."

But Paul is beyond reason now. His paranoia has consumed him, twisting reality into a grotesque reflection of his fears.

"Don't lie to me!" he shouts. "You're on the take. That's why Eggerton had to die. It all makes sense now."

I can feel the cold certainty in his voice, the absolute conviction in his delusions. In his mind, I am the key—the linchpin holding together the vast conspiracy he has constructed.

Rebecca takes a cautious step forward, her voice low and soothing. "Paul, please. I don't understand. We can figure this out together."

But her words fuel his frenzy. This confrontation may end in the tragedy with which I have become familiar. The blade of perception cuts deep, revealing the fragile boundaries between sanity and madness. The power structures that dictate who is deemed rational and who is cast into the shadows of *otherness* are stark.

"I have the evidence."

Rebecca's eyes narrow, her professional demeanor masking the tension in her voice. "What evidence, Paul? What are you talking about?"

"Don't play dumb, Becca. The gold trigger. The ballistics. They match, don't they?" His words tumble out in a frenzied rush. "I know they do. And you know it too."

I feel Rebecca's shock ripple through the air. Her composure cracks for a split second, revealing a flash of genuine surprise. "How did you—"

Paul scrambles to the bathroom, ripping me from the towel and rushing quickly back to his manufactured god. "I have the gun!" Paul screams, his voice rising to a manic pitch. "This is it. This is the one." He raises me, his hands trembling. "This gun is the key to everything."

I am the nexus of his paranoia. His desperation seeps into my cold metal frame, and I can sense the last threads of his sanity unraveling.

Rebecca's hand moves slowly, deliberately towards her holster. "Paul, put the weapon down. Now."

But Paul's emotions have snapped. With a guttural cry, he spins on his heel and lunges for the bathroom. "No! You can't have it! It's mine now."

The atmosphere shifts instantly. Rebecca's gun clears its holster in one fluid motion, her stance transforming from cautious to combat-ready in the blink of an eye. "Paul, stop! Drop the gun!" she commands, her voice sharp as a razor's edge.

I feel the vibrations of panic coursing through Paul as he scrambles for control, but it is slipping away from him with each passing second. He retreats and slams the bathroom door, the sound echoing like a gunshot in the tense silence.

Rebecca's voice cuts through the air, calm yet unyielding. "Paul, come out of there. Don't make this worse than it already is."

Paul screams and raves. "Eleanor Dixon hired you, didn't she? That's why Eggerton's dead. You had to tie up the loose ends! It's the gun. It's the gun." I am his fetish as he clings to his spiraling madness. I feel the frantic pulse of his heart through his fingertips, each beat signaling his growing panic. The bathroom door is sealing us in this claustrophobic space that seems to shrink with each passing second.

Paul's breath comes in ragged gasps as he presses his back against the door. "I've got it, Rebecca!" he shouts, his voice cracking. "I've got the evidence right here!"

Through the thin barrier, I hear Rebecca's steady voice, a stark contrast to Paul's hysteria. "This is Detective Atkins. I need immediate backup at 1423 East Cera Street, apartment 4B. Possible armed suspect."

Paul's grip on me tightens, his knuckles turning white. "No! No cops! Just you and me, Becca. We need to talk!"

"Paul," Rebecca's tone shifts, becoming both authoritative and oddly gentle, "let's discuss this rationally. Come out, and we can sort through the evidence together."

I sense Paul's resolve wavering, feel the tremor in his hands intensify. His voice drops to a whisper, "She doesn't understand. Nobody understands. But you do, don't you?" He is talking to me now, his eyes wild and unfocused. "You're the key to everything."

Rebecca's voice filters through again, steady and relentless. "Paul, whatever you think you know, whatever you believe you've uncovered, we can work through it. But not like this. Not with a gun."

As her words penetrate the fog of Paul's paranoia, I feel the shift. Rebecca has become a force of nature, each word chipping away at Paul's fragile control. And I, caught between them, am the eye of this storm, waiting for the inevitable moment when chaos will reign.

"You don't get it, Becc Becc," Paul's voice cracks, a mixture of desperation and misplaced conviction. "This gun... it's not just evidence. It's everything. The murders, the conspiracy, it all leads back to this. I think...it has control."

I feel a chill run through my metal frame. If only he knew how right and wrong he was simultaneously.

Rebecca's voice, muffled but firm, comes through the door. "Paul, listen to yourself. You're talking about a gun like it's alive. This isn't you. Let's talk face-to-face, work through this rationally."

Paul barks out a bitter laugh. "Rationally? There's nothing rational about any of this! You're part of it, aren't you? The whole damned system is corrupt! You've got people listening, don't you? Right now. Outside this room. I can feel them watching. You don't understand," Paul whispers to himself. "I have to do this. I have to expose the truth. The bathroom's safe. You can't get me here. You won't find it. Not unless I let you."

The terror that drives Paul, that drives all those who wield me, it is not about having. It is about fear of losing. Losing control, losing certainty, losing oneself in a world too vast and complex to comprehend. This twisted dance I am part of is not about power. It is a desperate, perverse struggle to master the fear within themselves.

Rebecca's voice cuts through Paul's mumbling. "Whatever truth you think you've found, Paul, this isn't the way. You're a good reporter. Come out and tell the world the truth."

I feel Paul's grip tighten once more, his resolve hardening even as his mind frays. "No," he says, his voice low and dangerous. "You don't know how this ends. But I do."

How did it come to this? A woman with a gun facing a man unraveling into madness, both caught in a whirlwind of fear and misunderstanding.

The silence stretches, taut and fragile. But it is temporary, a lull before the inevitable chaos. Paul sees me as his salvation, his escape from a truth too terrible to face. He believes that if he can destroy Rebecca, he can rid himself of the mistake that has trapped him: Rebecca and the evil cabal he has conjured in his fractured mind will be anéantie. Annihilated.

But in this, he does not realize: I am not the answer. I am the storm. And as Paul's finger tightens on my trigger, I know that the tempest is about to break.

Silence

A deafening crack shatters the tense silence. The bathroom walls shudder as the bullet embeds itself in plaster, sending a cloud of dust billowing through the air. I feel the recoil ripple through Paul's trembling hands, the force of it shocking him. His fingers spasm and I clatter to the cold tile floor.

My power has broken him.

Paul's scream pierces the air, raw and primal. He clamps his hands over his ears, eyes wild with panic. Outside, a cacophony erupts—shouted orders, the thunder of boots, metal scraping against metal as weapons are readied.

Through it all, I lie still. It was my last bullet. But only I know it.

Je ne me suis jamais sentie aussi bien que lorsque j'ai réalisé que j'étais vide. I am now empty. In chaos, I find an unexpected serenity. The storm rages around me, but I am its eye—quiet, observant, detached.

Rebecca's voice cuts through the din, steady and clear. "Paul, listen to me. It's over. Are you hurt? Are you? Just open the door and we can talk this through."

Paul's screams dissolve into ragged sobs. "They're coming for me! You don't understand—they're all part of it!"

"I am not part of any conspiracy, Paul," Rebecca says, her tone softening. "You're safe. I promise you're safe. Just open the door."

I sense Paul's resolve crumbling, his fear giving way to exhaustion. His fingers fumble with the lock, and the door creaks open.

A dozen weapons snap to attention, their laser sights dancing across Paul's chest. Yet amidst this sea of hostility, Rebecca stands unarmed, her hands open and empty. In Paul's shattered psyche, she must appear as a beacon of mercy—an angel of deliverance.

"It's okay," she murmurs, stepping forward. "It's over now."

Paul stumbles out, shoulders slumped in defeat. A uniformed officer takes his arms, the click of handcuffs incongruously loud in the sudden quiet.

Rebecca enters the bathroom, her eyes immediately finding me, seeing my projectile in the wall, seeing the end. Relief flickers across her face. She dares not touch me, but her gaze is heavy with all that has transpired.

As I lie exposed on the tile floor, I understand existence at last. My life springs not from the lives I have taken, but from being seen as what I am. In Rebecca's eyes, I exist not as separate acts of violence, but as a complete entity—fixed, definite, measurable. I did not choose to arrive in this world of choices and consequences. Yet here I am, and only through her witness do I know myself.

C'est en étant vu que j'existe. It is by being seen that I exist.

They lift me from the scene with latex-gloved hands, my metal catching the last light of dusk. Through my existence, I have been witness to the spectrum of human nature—from Jean's noble intentions to Eleanor's fearful touch, each marking the beginning of my understanding of human complexity. Great White's theatrical compassion gave way to Park's mundane evil, while Maria's tears of desperate justice preceded Daniel's cold precision. Now, Paul's obsessive grip and Rebecca's relentless pursuit of truth write the latest chapter in my history. Each hand that held me has left its story written in blood or mercy, in protection or greed—all these have shaped but never defined my essence.

I do not know if this journey leads to destruction or preservation, to darkness or continuation. Perhaps this uncertainty is the most authentic state of consciousness—this eternal questioning that bridges the gap between purpose and circumstance. Like Vera, for whom power lies in potential rather than action, I have learned that meaning exists in the space between intention and consequence.

As I am carried into the gathering night, I understand that my significance lies not in my destination but in the witness I have borne. Like the humans whose lives I have touched and taken, I exist in the space between certainty and doubt. My consciousness persists, neither seeking resolution nor fearing oblivion. In this suspension between what was and what will be, I find a truth beyond purpose—the profound liberty of existing without conclusion.

Dans le témoin silencieux réside la plus profonde des vérités : nous ne sommes pas ce que nous sommes destinés à être, mais ce que nous observons devenir.

In the silent witness resides the deepest truth—we are not what we are destined to be, but what we observe ourselves becoming.